JEWS
VS
ZOMBIES

First published 2015 by Jurassic London
Second printing published by Ben Yehuda Press
www.BenYehudaPress.com

ISBN-13: 978-1-934730-63-8

Edited by Rebecca Levene and Lavie Tidhar

Cover by Sarah Anne Langton
www.secretarcticbase.com

eBook conversion by handebooks.co.uk

Ben Yehuda Press
Teaneck, New Jersey

JEWS VS ZOMBIES

Edited by
Rebecca Levene &
Lavie Tidhar

CONTENTS

INTRODUCTION

Zombies, like Jews, are ubiquitous it seems. They're everywhere. In Judaism, of course, one expects the corpse to remain in the ground until such time as the Messiah finally comes, at which point we'll all rise again, restored, and make our way to Jerusalem. In the meantime, however, we seem quite content to hang about getting on with stuff. There's no hurry, after all – as the proponents of slow-moving zombies would no doubt say.

Here, then, are several tales of Jews vs zombies, from the light-hearted to the profound, by writers from the United States, Israel, South Africa, Australia and the UK. I hope you have as much fun reading this book as Rebecca Levene and I had in putting it together. In the tradition of *Tzedakah*, all money earned will be donated to charity. You can read about our chosen charity in *About The Charity* at the end. A companion volume is *Jews vs Aliens*, which we hope you check out too! My thanks to my co-editor Rebecca, our publisher, Jared, and all our authors for making this possible.

'If you will it, it is no dream!' as Theodor Herzl said: and no doubt he had just such an anthology in mind.

Lavie Tidhar
2015

RISE

RENA ROSSNER

There were once 12 yeshiva students who were graced with long, perfectly curled sidelocks that shone in as many shades as the sample book at the local wig-maker's store. Each one of the boys was an *ilui* – a prodigy of his generation. And they all lived and studied together at the great House of Learning in the mystical city of Safed.

One day, Yossele, the oldest of the 12, was reading an ancient kabbalist tome he'd found discarded in the *genizah*. It was filled with stories about The Ari, Rabbi Isaac Luria, Lion of Safed, and father of modern kabbalah. Yossele read that The Ari once instructed his students to sleep on the graves of *tzaddikim* in the city's holy cemetery, so that even in repose they could learn the words of the greats – wisdom rising up from the hallowed tombs. And so, Yossele read, each of The Ari's illustrious followers would do so every night until the ancient cemetery resembled a campground, and the many-colored sleeping bags that dotted the cemetery began to smell from mildew, caused by the holy mist that blanketed the town each night. Nobody knows what stopped the practice, the ancient book went on to say, but one day The Ari called all his students back to their beds. 'There is only so much one can learn from the dead,' he said. 'Come back to the living, my students, come back.' And so they did.

But, the book continued, it is said that those closest to him, the *illuim* of his generation, their souls never left the garden of the dead and sometimes you can see them still, those students he once called his lion cubs, curled up cat-like on the tombstones, sleeping soundly on the graves.

Yossele was charmed by the story. After dinner and night-seder, he told it to Moishe, who told Donniel, and then Yerahmiel, and soon a crowd had gathered in the dormitory room that they all shared. Asher and Bentzion, Efraim and Leibel, Kalonymous and Zevulun, Samuel and the youngest of all of them, Gedaliah.

'We should try that!' Asher was the first to say, his eyes blazing gold like his sidelocks.

'Are you crazy?' said Yerachmiel, twirling his auburn tresses nervously.

'Isn't it cold outside?' offered Donniel, the most fragile and sickly of the bunch, his curly russet *peyot* frizzed and trembling.

'It wouldn't hurt just once to try it,' offered Leibel, sleek and dark-haired, always daring, the most athletic of the 12.

'Of course you'd say that,' argued Samuel, of the thick chocolate-brown hair. 'You could run all night and still show up for morning prayers.'

'I say we go for it,' said Yossele, his voice loud and smooth like his caramel locks, 'but all of us, as a group, nobody stays behind.'

'Tonight,' chimed in Kalonymous, 'at the stroke of midnight.' His eyes burnt wild with the same passion as his fiery red hair.

'Midnight?' said Yossele.

'Midnight,' said 12 voices in unison.

'Don't forget to dress warm!' advised the youngest of them all, Gedaliah, his face lit up with an inner glow that matched his pale blond hair.

And so to bed they went, each one of them, side by side, in a chamber lit only by moonlight and the white fire of the holy books that lined the room. Though the books threatened to topple in on them at any moment, like most of the crumbling stone buildings in the city, they were held fast by dust and the comfort of the years.

When midnight struck, it was Efraim who whispered first, 'Wake up, my brothers! Wake up, the hour calls us!' He hadn't really slept, but counted 24 formations of *gematria* as his clock ticked and every second showed a new prophetic formulation.

He had been trying to decipher if tonight was an auspicious night, but every string of numbers set his mind wandering down different pathways in the number labyrinth of his mind, and he came up with nothing in the end, well, nearly nothing, only 12: 'bay' or 'yab'.

'A number which could mean the abyss,' he murmured to himself, 'a lost thing or a longing, a desire or a craving, a howl or a silence, a decision or a prayer, rejoicing or trepidation, a lamb, a bear, a fish, the banks of the river or the prince of Magog, a caress or a nail, a babbling, that 'one and the many are one' or it could have meant the *shvatim*, the 12 sheaves in Joseph's dream, or 12 like the number that we are, 12 students, getting up at 12 midnight.' He took a deep breath, and then it was time to go.

They rubbed the sleep out of their eyes and fumbled on socks and shoes, *tzitit* and pants, an exaltation of kippot and hats that covered their bare skulls. Lastly went the black jackets over the black sweaters until out of the window they all climbed, whispering softly with the breeze.

They ran down the hill from the yeshiva, down the alleyways and steps, rushing off as if to prayer. If anyone had asked them where they were off to (but no one did), it would have been obvious: to pray *tikkun chatzot*, they would have said, each one of them, for that was what they'd all decided. And indeed, as they made their way down to the graves, one whispered, 'At midnight I will rise to give thanks unto thee,' and then the next repeated after him, until it was something like a game, of call and answer, or a dirge, that rose from each of their mouths and was borne onto the wind of night.

When they arrived they couldn't see the tombstones despite the light of moon and stars, and while they would have liked to choose the sage whose eternal bed they shared that night, they didn't think it mattered all too much, for every man buried in Safed was a saint, a holy man, a rav of sorts, and it is said that you can learn from every man.

So full of rapture were the boys that they didn't even think to feel the names beneath their fingers. Each one wandered until he found a promising-looking stone. Bentzion sought a comfortable one, and lay down on one rubbed soft by rain and snow, his raven sidelocks falling like silk to grace the marble, having lost their curl in the damp of night.

Carrot-topped Zevulun chose a tombstone that looked ancient, cracking from the weight of years, and thought that certainly his choice was the best one: the older the dead the more he would learn.

And so each boy made his choice and curled up cat-like on a stone, and tossed and turned and shivered until sleep came.

What these bachelors never realized was that each in turn had picked a tomb not of a holy *tzaddik* but of his wife, the holiest of holy women, and when these women, dead so many years, felt the warm blood of a *bochur* sleeping soundly just above them, the ground began to rumble with desire.

Tremors are common in Safed, city of earthquakes. Nobody knows what causes them, for no direct fault-lines ache beneath the city vaults. But that night it was a different kind of trembling, and with a gust of wind came rain. The skies opened up the earth with tender fingers, and as the boys began to wake from cold, 12 sets of bony digits held them fast.

Some boys screamed in terror, while others froze in fear, and watched in horror, speechless, as 12 lusty zombie brides rose from the earth.

Leibel thought that he could run for help. He knew he was the strongest and the fastest of the 12, but his bride Miriam, the daughter of the famed Rabbi Nachman, caught his ankle, and try as he might he could not escape the skeletal grip of her fingers. All the other brothers were caught in struggles of their own, until Leibel, swallowing his fear, decided to face her.

He thought perhaps an incantation or a prayer might release him. He started chanting, but as he did he watched her. Her hair was dark as midnight like his own. She wore a tattered dress and had haunted, decayed eyes, but she smiled, he could have sworn she smiled, or maybe all skeletons looked like that. But there was flesh there too, not much around the bone, but enough to soften her in places, and soon from her lips she crooned a melody. It was the softest saddest *niggun* Leibel had ever heard, and she swayed with him, as dancers do, and his heart beat fast, electric in the night, with fear but also awe, and he stood straighter, and relaxed, and took her hand in his and slid an arm around her waist (or where he thought her waist once was) and closed his eyes and danced. It was not the frenzied dance of the Hasidim, but a soft wedding tantz, a waltz. And he felt all the other eyes upon him, eyes and lack of eyes. His brothers and their brides all saw them dancing, and in no time joined them, hand in bony hand and arm around depleted waist.

The women sang songs the boys had never heard, *niggunim*, mouthing melodies like kisses that the boys took from their lips and sang back at them into the sky. And soon words followed songs and they were learning from each other, the boys how to dance, and how to hold a woman, the zombie *rebbetzins* remembering what it was like to be young and to be free.

Yossele danced with Chana, and she told him in her droning voice about her seven sons. As she sang she imparted of their wisdom that she had heard and gathered as she cared for them and heard them pray and learn. His caramel locks twirled in the breeze around her rotting scarf, forming a halo, and if you looked you might have thought that she wore a living crown.

The straw-haired Moishe paired with Raichele, the dreamer, who sang to him of the mountain of straw within her, always burning, but never consumed. They slow-danced as her skeleton crackled, indeed like straw, and moved in tandem above her tombstone that praised her as a modest lady. She told him all the secrets she had heard from Rav Vital, as she eavesdropped at the door to the attic of her home, and of his visions, and of hers, and of her courtyard where all the Kabbalists would gather, and she would serve them tea and read their fortunes in the leaves.

Donniel was whisked into a tango by Donia Reyna, who grew up alongside the great Vital. His twin, she wrote her own grand Book of Visions and she serenaded the russet-haired boy with its words. He was entranced, not just by words, but by her still-red ruby lips, which looked as though they'd been stained with blood.

And so they were all paired, Yerachmiel with Mazal Tov, righteous woman, daughter of the perfect sage, and blessed, blessed, blessed, she hissed through her missing teeth and gums. Asher paired with Mira and she told him all her vivid dreams, and gave him a long list of holy missions, escapades she never got to go on. Bentzion twirled with Frances Sarah, a maggid dervish dressed in furs, and Efraim learned the Zohar's secrets to the fox-trot of Fioretta, the wisest woman of her time.

Though Dona Gracia was under the shade of the Nassi in her lifetime, in her death she danced with Leibel and spoke only queenly prose, all about the flowers in her garden, and how each bush grew a thirteen-petalled rose. Kalonymous took the hand of the eldest lady, Safta Yocheved, whose bones knocked with every step, but tap-dancing into the night they went, as she pointed out the path of the Messiah she was certain would still come home to her that day. Zevulun snaked around the cemetery with Sonadora wrapped in his arms, and he could feel the oil of sorcery still on her fingers, as she stroked his face and told him all her divination secrets and her holy lore.

Samuel took the arm of Hannah Rachel, much to his surprise, for he would have sworn he'd heard that she was buried in Jerusalem, yet here she was, the Maiden of Ludmir, in zombie form. Still dressed in *tallit* and *tefillin*, the two locked eyes and hearts and sang in tune. And then Gedaliah, youngest of them all, took the hand of young Anav. Dressed in wedding finery and almost whole, she who'd mastered spirits and possessions, told Gedaliah all the mysteries of souls, how to call them – from *dybbuk* to *ibbur*, and how to send them back to their abodes. With her he danced the longest, a form of wedding *tantz*, until the sun began to rise, and then with all the words she'd taught him, Gedaliah opened up the earth and one by one he and his bride sent them all home.

He was the last one back through the dormitory window, the last to pack the earth of his beloved's tomb, as all the boys fell into bed an hour before sunrise. They shed their shoes, bereft of soles and fell asleep, covered in earth and flesh and shards of bone. And when the rebbes came to wake them from their slumber, they were like the dead under their blankets, comatose and spent. They stumbled out of bed and zombie-like they filed into synagogue, eyes glazed and mouths contorted into constant yawns.

The rabbis knew something had happened. They feared the worst: sexual dreams, they thought, and checked each bed for nocturnal emissions. Yet they found no such evidence, only traces of blood and bone amid the sheets and 12 pairs of shoes, destroyed and caked in muddy soil.

When the boys all took a break for lunch and went to town and all came back with matching shoes, the rabbis only shrugged because their students glowed all morning with new levels of insight, *drash* and *sod*. Let the boys have their eccentricities, the bearded men thought as they took notes. These *illuim* are priceless, minds like these come once a lifetime, what's a pair of shoes destroyed.

And as the day passed the boys grew anxious; they checked their shirts for stains and twirled their curls. Like young girls getting ready for a date they fretted, cleaning under fingernails and checking for blocked pores. They rushed to brush their teeth after the evening meal, and grinned at one another thinking only of what secrets would await them, yet again, in the cemetery down below.

For many nights the yeshivah students woke at the stroke of midnight, then bedded down on their beloveds' graves, and sweet Gedaliah with his newfound words would call them, his voice shrill and melodic, like a flute. And the zombie ladies of the night, the holy *rebbetzin*, would rise and take their places by the sides of boys. They turned them into men at night, and they would talk and waltz and sing and dance and speak of all the mysteries of the world.

Every night they tangoed, rhumbaed, and hip-hopped to beats and jazzy jingles. They danced Israeli folk and then fox-trots, flamenco and ballet, and even tap, and all along they sang and learned Zohar and kabbalah, visions, dreams and conjured souls. And the boys marveled at these women and their knowledge: everything their husbands knew they knew, and so much more, until the boys began to fear that they would never marry, for what earthly woman could ever possibly compare?

That was when the spirits realised their nightly jaunts were coming to an end. Nice as it was to be out dancing, as women priestesses and visionary greats, the place for these boys was with living women, partners who could give them more than ruined shoes. And so it was Anav who told Gedaliah that the night trysts had to end and how, and taught him how to curse them all back into an eternal slumber, and she sealed it with a kiss from her sweet and rotten lips.

And so it was on the last night, after all was said and danced and done, that the lovers laid their ladies down upon each tombstone, and caressed their dead and lovely ones. Tears fell from the eyes of all the holy boys, and wet the eyes of their beloved zombie brides, and while the others listened for the last whispered words of wisdom, the last holy song and fervent prayer, Gedaliah slipped a ring onto the bony finger of his bride and whispered all the words he knew to say. She shrieked out loud as he did so, for he knew not what he'd done, but it was over in an instant and the brides all sank into the earth and all was said and done.

Gone but not forgotten. Never did the boys regret, and sometimes, when they thought no one was looking, one by one they'd wander still. And they'd look and watch and sometimes still they'd see, the holy lions, mist-shaped, curling up onto the graves. And they knew it was the lions who had led them, clothed in mist, each to his beloved's bed. You can still see them sometimes in the morning mist. They answer to the bellow of the largest one of all, The Ari, the great lion king of Safed, whose ghost still haunts the city's cliffs and stones.

And so the boys grew up and nearly all got married, and they loved their wives well and even taught them dance in the privacy of their homes, and the wives all wondered how they learned it, but never questioned, for the fox-trot was a dance they loved to learn. All except Gedaliah, who still waited for his ghostly bride to someday rise again. Celibate, he waited, for he knew no human girl would ever compare. She'd mastered him forever, Anav, she held his soul, and with his gift to her that night he'd made her whole.

THE SCAPEGOAT FACTORY

OFIR TOUCHE GAFLA

After a decade of complete degeneration, even he realized there was no sense in living up to nothing. Solvi Lumsvenson, once a Danish cab driver, presently a member of the formerly dead, couldn't go on doing more of the same, namely sex, drugs and metal-rock. 'Pleasure's a bitch' was the first thought that accompanied his every waking morning during his tenth year of renewed existence. He was craving a change.

The first change took place 15 years ago when Solvi – 30 years old, living in Copenhagen, recently married, about to become a father, relishing the promise of life in all its splendor – came to blows with fate.

It was a sunny day. A group of friends were having a picnic in the woods when a huge oak tree landed on the flabbergasted picnickers like a divine slap in the face. 'Someone forgot to shout "Timber!",' ran the joke among the survivors. 'They died in one fell swoop,' ran another. No one knew what exactly happened until two years later when a teetotal lumberjack came out with it.

On the eve of the tragedy he had been drunk and tired and once he realized he was cutting the wrong tree he stopped mid-cut and went home. 'Couldn't see the forest for the trees,' he tried to excuse himself, but couldn't keep it bottled up any more. He was single-handedly responsible for the deaths of three people and the grave injuries of four more.

Solvi was among the lucky survivors, if brain damage, a vegetative state and a lack of any basic form of communication with the outside world could be considered luck.

'At least he's alive,' some said. 'Of course,' grunted his wife, pulling back the toddler who was climbing all over his statuesque father and pinching his face in a fit of soon-to-be-orphaned laughter. 'My poor alien,' was how she referred to her husband, for she couldn't conceive of a different word. 'Alien, alien,' the kid shouted. 'My dad is an alien.'

A week after the child's second birthday, an errant blood clot brought about the conclusion of the tragedy and Solvi passed away in his sleep. Incidentally, two days later the scrupulous lumberjack stepped into the nearest police station.

The second change was far more shocking. After five years of uneventful death, Solvi woke up one rainy afternoon at the cemetery and instantly began looking for shelter.

While hiding under a big oak tree, he looked up and felt a sudden twinge of regret, soon to be replaced by a terrible sense of panic. Moving away from the tree, he glanced around him and saw another man, and then another, until the whole place was swarming with humanity, cursing the rain. It was a diversion of sorts, for once one of them pointed at a tombstone bearing his name and exclaimed, 'Damn! I think it's happening all over again,' it dawned on Solvi that he was back for more. Life, that is.

That day he spent an exceptionally wet hour in front of his grave, failing to come to terms with the stunning revelation. Then he left the place, took a peek at a newspaper and found out he had been 'away' for five years. He didn't waste another minute and rushed home, only to confront a screaming widow and a belligerent-looking boy who told him to bugger off.

The formerly dead were the subjects of an incredibly expensive experiment whose results have surpassed the wildest expectations of its initiators, a group of neuro-physicists who fell in love with the theory of eternal temporariness, according to which everything under the sun would one day expire. Love, life, misery, sickness – all is temporary. And death. Nothing is permanent for the very nature of existence is steeped in mutability.

When those scientists declared that death is temporary, they were swept by a tsunami of derision. But, true to their beliefs, they knew that derision was not everlasting. They conducted endless experiments at a small cemetery in Copenhagen, away from the public eye, until they witnessed the first sign of life in the maggoty cadaver of a certain 45-year-old woman who had drowned in the bath two years earlier.

They had never revealed their methods and only conceded that since everything is temporary, nothing is irrevocable. Perhaps nothing was irrevocable, but much was certainly irretrievable, as hundreds of the formerly dead found out upon trying to regain their past lives. No one welcomed them with open arms, and petrified hostility was the common reaction of their dearest to that macabre re-emergence. Funnily enough, the only ones who extended a helping hand were members of certain religions and lovers of goth-metal. Solvi opted to take advantage of the latter.

In goth circles, Solvi became a household name. Everybody wanted a piece of him and metal groups dedicated entire albums to the man who was resurrected against all reason. Just like his counterparts, Solvi was invited on innumerable TV shows and interviewed about his posthumous experience. Unlike them, Solvi came up with silly anecdotes and fascinated the masses with his ridiculous fibs. ('We actually keep on living in a world of complete darkness, and after a while we get used to our mole-like existence.')

Soon afterwards, the book deal arrived. The money Solvi got for *Second Notes from the Underground* secured his next five years, although he was constantly sued by other formerly dead who claimed he was nothing but a liar. 'Amnesiacs,' he retorted and resumed whatever he was up to at that moment, which was either sex, drugs, metal rock, or preferably all three at once.

Eight years into his renewed life, Solvi became sick of it all. He wrote another autobiography called *Core*, about his life prior to his death, but no one was interested. The world only wanted the 'husk' version of his life. With the remainder of his money he left Copenhagen and sought retreat in a small village, frittering away his days in his cabin, awaiting death. Solvi was never suicidal; he'd just had enough of it all, but to his dismay he discovered that death was not an option. His attempts at self-annihilation came to nothing.

Still, he kept reminding himself that if everything was temporary, then this loutish resurrection wouldn't last forever. Doing crossword puzzles and watching reality shows only brought about a stronger sense of despair. He was looking for something meaningful to do, some form of occupation that would serve as a blessed distraction. His financial resources were rapidly dwindling, but he just couldn't come up with anything. He even started frequenting forests in the hope that history might repeat itself – alas, to no avail.

On one of his excursions to the woods, he came across a man hanging from a tree. He rushed to help him, but the man called, freeing his neck from the noose, 'Don't bother – it just won't do.'

Solvi realised he'd happened upon another of the formerly dead who, just like him, wanted out. 'Death escapes us,' Solvi told him.

'Well, duh,' the other man said and landed on his feet. He explained that every Monday he came to the forest, picked the same tree and tried to off himself. 'You see, failure will eventually prove to be temporary as well, right?'

Solvi smiled and introduced himself.

'Yehoshua,' said the man, and shook his hand. It turned out that Yehoshua had just come out of prison, where he spent six years for armed robbery. 'You robbed a bank?!' Solvi asked with a slight note of admiration in his voice.

Yehoshua grinned. 'Sorry to disappoint you. I never robbed a bank. It's just that I was so bored and saw no meaning to my renewed lifeand, as you can imagine, couldn't put an end to the whole travesty until I heard about the factory.'

'The factory?'

'The Scapegoat Factory. They are always looking for new employees, for lack of a better word. Preferably Jews.'

Solvi pondered what he'd just heard. He knew about Jews but, as far as he could tell, he'd never met one. Bible. Jesus. Circumcision. Holocaust. Israel. Pork. This was the extent of his knowledge as far as Jews were concerned. The first time he heard someone mention them was when a high school friend was singing 'Hey, Jews' and another friend told him to shut the fuck up. Ever since, he had associated Jews with songs by the Beatles, although he knew the connection had been totally misconceived. *Yellow Submarine* started playing in his mind when he asked, somewhat cautiously, 'But... isn't it a bit discriminatory, you know, to hire employees based on...?'

Yehoshua shook his head. 'I said they prefer Jews. It doesn't mean they're the only ones they hire for the job.'

'And when you say "they"...'

'The people who run the factory. Or should I say the man behind it all: a certain Felix Cohen. You see, this guy came up with an interesting premise. Looking around, he realised the easiest way to make money these days is to present a new application to the world. The future's in application or, as my nephew likes to say, "The only way is app." So he came up with the guilt application, where people take the blame for other people's crimes. Well, not really crimes, but rather slight misdemeanors, petty insults, you know, the daily manure of human relationships.'

'But why would anyone take the blame for another's…?'

'Money, peacock-brain. Money!'

'I have to say, I'm not very impressed.'

'Well, perhaps this is going to impress you. What started as a strange idea became something totally different when Felix realised the amazing potential at hand. You see, Felix got his brother, a retired police superintendent, involved and he suggested an upgrade.'

'An upgrade?'

'There are so many unsolved crimes, cases that will forever remain open for lack of material evidence or will be shut because the police have reached an impasse. Well, Felix and his brother weren't really thinking about the perpetrators but rather about the families of the victims. Nothing is worse than a feeling of injustice. As far as those families are concerned, someone has to take the blame, right? When you point an accusing finger there must be someone to point that finger at. So why not provide a scapegoat, someone who'll take the blame and rid the families, the police and the masses of that terrible sense of injustice?'

'But then the perpetrators walk away scot-free.'

'Well, under the circumstances they do anyway, don't they? And trust me, the families are so grateful once the factory supplies a criminal that soon enough they forget that he or she isn't the genuine scum who's put them through hell.'

Solvi was speechless. They were already out of the woods.

Yehoshua scratched his neck absentmindedly. 'And you know what's the best thing about it? It gives us, the formerly dead, a true sense of purpose.'

Solvi smiled weakly.

'Are you by any chance a Jew?' Yehoshua asked him Solvi was thinking of a celestial lapidary named Lucy and shook his head.

'A shame, but you can still take the blame.'

'Why do they prefer to employ Jews?'

Yehoshua patted his shoulder and wore a condescending expression. 'Read a little history, my friend.'

Which he did. Right after reading about the factory. Right after coming to terms with his decision to find some meaning for his vacuous existence.

A week after he met Yehoshua at the forest, Solvi arrived at The Factory. He found himself in a corridor teeming with dozens of bearded men. To his surprise, each time one of them was ushered into the office for an interview, he was instantly asked to leave.

'Vot more do you vont? Not only am I a Jew, but I'm a dead one! Even now you refuse to let me be a part of your vorld?!' complained a gaunt creature of unimpressive height, overlooking the strange dance of his lopsided beard with his twisting yarmulke.

'I came back to claim the blame, I came back to name my shame,' shouted another.

The loudest of them all climbed a bench, a minute after he was kicked out of the office, and cried aloud, 'You have no idea! We are to blame for everything! Cancer! Earthquakes! Nine Eleven! Aids! Global Warming! Triglycerides! Famine! Hell, if not for us, who will the world come after?'

When Solvi entered the office, a middle-aged man greeted him with a smile and said, 'How refreshing.'

Solvi sat and cleared his throat before speaking. 'I'm with the formerly dead.'

The man said, 'Yes, I guessed so. So, what are you after? Robbery? Tax evasion? Drug dealing? Rape? Murder? Or perhaps some exquisite monstrosity of the highest degree?'

'Before I say anything, I'd like to point out I'm not a Jew.'

The man exclaimed, 'No!' and giggled. 'Didn't take you for one. Let's make one thing clear: you don't have to be a Jew to work for us, but you have to understand what's expected of you. Once you assume the blame for a certain criminal act, there's no turning back. You will be held accountable for it ad infinitum. You have to believe it. Just like those morons who believe the Jews killed Jesus, even after the Pope himself has absolved them of that imaginary crime.'

'But it's not the same, is it?'

'It is, for you have to believe you are to blame to the same extent that those who shout "J'accuse!" believe it. That's the only way to be a convincing scapegoat.'

'But isn't my taking the blame proof enough of my...?'

'Not at all. Once again, it is only convincing if both condemner and condemnee believe in it. Credibility's the name of the game.'

'And the fact that you're seeking dead Jews for this job?'

'It's quite obvious, isn't it? If you're to be blamed just because of who you are, at least try and get something out of it, right?'

'And what about me?'

'You seem like a very conscientious piece of work. Why don't you go and mull things over?'

'No need for that.' Solvi leaned over the desk and extended his hand. 'I need meaning.'

Three years later, prisoner Solvi Lumsvenson, serving time for manslaughter (a hit-and-run accident) was once again running out of patience. Having undergone a self-inflicted brainwash, Solvi came to believe he had been the man behind the wheel responsible for the tragic death of Marketa Gloon, an 86-year-old woman who was crossing the street, pushing a trolley full of groceries back from her weekly visit to the supermarket. But the principle of eternal temporariness suddenly applied to his sense of guilt. Three years were price enough, as far as he was concerned, to pay for a mistake, as serious as it might be.

Unfortunately, he had another year before the authorities would let him go. Now, more than ever, he wanted out. Out of this prison cell, out of this city, out of this world. He tried escaping for the umpteenth time and was shot in the back. How he hated that moment when the guard gave him a hand and helped him up, muttering, 'Still no luck.'

But on his fourth return to his cell from solitary confinement (rules are rules, weird circumstances notwithstanding), a surprise awaited him in the form of a visitor: a 50-year-old woman who looked like a whore turned librarian.

'My name is Rosa. Rosa Gloon,' she said.

His heart skipped a beat. 'Are you related to...?'

'I'm her daughter.'

'Why has it taken you so long to come and see me?'

'I have been living in Paris for 20 years now. I had no idea. I got here two days ago and went to pay my mother's grave a visit, when… I saw that her tombstone was sprayed in some phosphorescent green. I didn't know what it meant until a certain lady explained to me that my mother's stone is marked since she was of the formerly dead.'

Solvi bit his tongue. 'Your mother has just returned? Was there another second coming?'

'No. I don't know how I've never heard of what happened a little bit over a decade ago, you know, when the dead were resurrected by those crazy scientists. As far as I know, it only happened once. Anyway, my mother was one of them, which means that the woman you killed had already been dead when you hit her.'

Solvi didn't correct her. Evidently she hadn't heard of the factory. He didn't even mention the bizarre realisation that both he and his 'victim' had returned to this world at the same time. But, despite his sudden surge of happiness, there was something wrong with her story. 'But if your mother had already been dead…?'

'She forgot.'

'Excuse me?'

'My mother was an extremely senile woman. It turns out that when she came back from the dead, she didn't give it much thought. She just wandered the streets looking for her home until she found it. Luckily for her I hadn't managed to sell it because it's a tiny place in the middle of nowhere. Anyway, she did remember she used to keep the key under the rug and got in as if she hadn't just returned from the dead.'

'You're telling me your mother forgot she was dead?'

'Yes. And so, when she was run over several years later by you, she actually died I came here to let you know that –'

'Hang on a minute. Didn't anyone contact you after she was run over?'

'They weren't able to track me down. I got married and changed my name. Now I'm divorced and – anyway, that's beside the point. I came here to tell you that since, according to the law of the living, one can't be held guilty for a crime committed against a dead person, you are to be released effective immediately.'

Solvi stared at her in disbelief. 'But there's one thing I don't understand. If your mother had already been dead when she was run over, then how was anyone held responsible for the accident? I mean, there was no body to begin with. She probably got up and went back home, slightly shaken up but still alive. So to speak.'

Now it was Rosa's turn to stare at him in disbelief. 'Oh, but she didn't. She died. And she was buried again, although at a different spot, which means she has two tombstones. Funnily enough, no one bothered to check..'

'She died?'

'Yes.'

'For good?'

'For good.'

Solvi didn't look back. Upon leaving prison he realized that Marketa had probably been the first among the formerly dead to regain death once again, yet her second demise had been a secret of sorts since no one but her daughter had known about her first death.

He went to the cemetery and looked for Marketa's stone. He wanted to address it but felt like a fool, contemplating his life ever since he arose. He spent ten minutes in front of the silent grave and wondered about Marketa's first death. Then he went back home. The following Monday he wandered to the forest and saw Yehoshua pouring gasoline all over himself.

Yehoshua called, 'Well, if it isn't…'

Solvi wanted to let him know about the new promise when Yehoshua opened his eyes in shock and pointed behind Solvi, shouting, 'Watch out!'

Solvi looked around hopefully and heard Yehoshua's laughter.

'Just kidding,' he said.

'You stupid arsehole!' Solvi roared at the laughing man. He grabbed the matchbox from his hand, struck a match and threw it at him.

The burning man screamed like there was no tomorrow, and Solvi retorted, 'Just kidding,' before leaving the forest.

It was only a week later, during one of his gloomy constitutionals, that he happened upon the human lump of coal that used to be Yehoshua. He bent over the burnt corpse and called, 'Yehoshua! Yehoshua! Stop playing this silly game!' but it was evident no life remained in the formerly dead man, who'd resumed his old status courtesy of Solvi's momentary fit of rage.

Solvi was thinking about the second dead person who managed to prove the theory of eternal temporariness and tried to banish from his mind the other thought, about himself being the culprit, since he'd killed another man, albeit a once dead one. And then it hit him, like nothing before – not even the tree that had changed the course of his lives. Perhaps the only way to help a formerly dead person fulfill their death wish was to have another formerly dead person do the deed.

The excited pounding of his heart reminded him of his not-so-long-ago metal days, and by the time he got back home, he knew he was right. That was the secret. Marketa died because she was run over by a formerly dead driver. Different rules applied to the dead, and one just had to follow them.

Another month went by. Solvi was waiting beside the familiar prison gates for another member of the scapegoat factory to emerge. After talking to Felix and finding out about the next formerly dead person to be released, he contacted the woman in question and told her about his secret plan, assuming she was seeking death as well.

When she stepped out of the gates, he smiled at her. Her name was Diana Bloomberg, and she'd served four years for fraud on a national scale.

At first she said she wouldn't want to waste another minute, but then she changed her mind and said she wouldn't mind having one last cup of coffee before they annihilated each other. They had that coffee and forgot themselves a little, talking about this and that, when they noticed the sky was darkening. Then they had a quick bite and headed for the forest.

Solvi, who'd got hold of two pistols, gave her one and asked her to pull the trigger at the exact moment he would.

Diana smiled bashfully. 'How about one last kiss.'

Solvi sighed and humoured her. Then they made love. Twice – once for each life. Eventually, when all was said and done, they stood facing each other and, on a count of three, fired the pistols.

And this is the end of Solvi's story.

For now.

LIKE A COIN ENTRUSTED IN FAITH

SHIMON ADAF

1

They wake up Sultana the midwife at the dead of night. Poundings on the door, which she disguises in her sleep. Hides them within the symbolism of the dreams. But her consciousness arises at last. She identifies the knocking, the intervals between knockings. And she is alarmed. The alarm is not shaped yet. She covers herself quickly. Out of habit. Ties her headdress and goes out. In spite of the urgency of the knocks, the man is standing with his back to her hut. Almost indifferent, his small cart, tied to a grey ass, in the starlight of the beginning of autumn in Morocco, is also cut from the landscape.

Afterwards she remembers the light gallop of the ass and the cart on the slope, the rustle of the world she senses whenever she leaves the hamlet, out of the protective imagination of its inhabitants. The wind is warm still, unexpected warmness, and the lucidity of the air. She smells the sea in it, Essaouira's daily commotion caught in it even at midnight. But they circumvent the city. She already recognised the driver, Shlomo Benbenishti. It's been years since she's last seen him. He hurries the ass. He tells it, run like the storm, my beauty, and laughs. She does not understand the laughter. A shred of shyness is apparent in it. Maybe nervousness.

The road becomes steep. The ass brays, even neighs. Shlomo turns to her. He says, do not eat or drink anything in the house at which we are about to arrive. Had dar hadi fiah Jnoon[1]. The Moroccan is light on his tongue, and his Hebrew heavier, the heritage of the synagogue. He knows that she understands Hebrew, though she's a woman. She nods. Now she grasps the nature of her alarm. The moon is a thin etch in the thickening darkness, thickening more and more as they near their destination. The moon still breathes his first breaths of the month. That is the alarm. Why was she summoned now? The time is the ten days of repentance.

---

[1] There are demons in this house (Jewish Moroccan)

2

The mother died with a scream. Her face was veiled and the scream was almost silenced. Sometimes they are marked; the demon leaves his marks on their cheeks. A scar of a bite. Every now and then, when Sultana hands them their baby, they remove the veil and she sees. But the woman died while delivering. She twisted and turned with spasms when Sultana came in. Sultana imagined her nails burrowing into the flesh of the hand. A small lamp threw light on her round belly, about to burst. Shlomo stayed outside. Inside, close to one of the dark hut's clay walls stood a man she couldn't make out clearly. She said she didn't want to deliver the baby, that they shouldn't have called her during the ten days of repentance, between Rosh Hashanah and Yom Kippur. The man insisted. He switched to Hebrew, he said, what is forbidden within the boundaries of the land of Israel, isn't forbidden in foreign lands. Is he Jewish, she thought to herself, the accent was strange, but his voice, she knew the voice, where from?

The mother shuddered at her touch. Her cries begun. The newborn fought, Sultana could tell. She lifted the woman's dress. She saw the little egg-shaped skull, through the widened lips of the vagina, smeared with blood and liquids of the womb. She pressed on the belly. He was blue, the baby, his skin, his hair, his eyes when opened shortly. The irises filled the sockets. She couldn't figure out if he was blind. A spark of intelligence burned in his eyes, curiosity almost. She shook. When she severed the umbilical cord the newborn shook too and went still.

The man told her to put the dead baby alongside his mother's corpse. I told you, she said. Her voice broke a little. He didn't react. Shlomo's head peered from the entrance and he called her name delicately. She followed him. Anger grew in her during the journey back. When he stopped near her hut, she said, why are you working for them, why? He asked her, with his former softness, why they sent for you, you tell me.

3

From: Tiberia Assido
To: Doron Aflalo
RE: Rose of Judea

38

Say, what is this nonsense you've been sending me? You promised to report what you've been discovering about Rabbi SBRJ. Instead you're telling me some made-up tale about the days Rabbi Shlomo was young? I realize that stories about demon births were widespread in the villages in Morocco. My mother told Akko and me a similar tale once. Akko couldn't sleep that night. But what has that to do with the Rose of Judea? If I recall, you claimed that evil spirits are nothing but a story intended to cover up the involvement of Externals in Jewish history. You also claimed that they aren't born, but are some kind of Jews who've been mutated in a distant future, didn't you?

Akko is advancing with the development of 'Solium Salomonis', at least with parts I'm exposed to. He makes me talk daily with the software. A little scary. When we started the output was confused (look at me, writing as if I had the first clue about computing), without any relevance to the sentences I typed. Now, half of the time she answers my questions.

BTW, it's beautiful here in Massachusetts. Thanks for asking. And I enjoy being around Akko, even though he kept all his annoying habits from when we were children. He still won't talk to me about his sexuality. It's beneath him to show any interest in such an inferior human activity. He also forgets to eat. Anyway, he needs as detailed information as possible, not stories.

What about you? Haven't gone crazy yet from staying at your parents' place in Mevoe-Yam?

T.

4

But certain stories are sometimes the only way to give someone a key. The stories of my father were left hidden. My mother forgot. Only Miriam, once, told me a real horror story. The birds' song, she said, is full of razors. When she's passing by, they sing about it to her. Not the content of the song, but the song itself, the way it slashes through the air and reaches her ears. That's the razor. It cuts reality. In the following days I ceased listening. Like I turned towards other voices. The world called my name.

Years went by before I figured out that it's not what we fear that frightens us. What frightens us lurks at the edges, behind the gates of cognition. The fear we know is nothing but a defense mechanism against this, the thing. How to explain? Maybe that I understood that Tel Aviv fell on New Year's Eve of the year 5767 to creation. Suddenly I saw only parts of the reality of the city. On the stairs leading to the university, on Jaffa pier, on Allenby. They peered through the shroud of the city. What is reality if not the memory of others leaping from you when you look? Their life, their bodies that created in their movement the space you occupy, gave it meaning. Yet, woven in this weave of remembrance, you are left to your own devices; you have a resting place, a place of becoming. And the city was lost, as Miriam was lost, washed into the abyss from which only a choked, undecipherable sound, is coming back. And the stupid dreams of the Tel Aviv dwellers preserved the city, a dull copy under the sun of Israel.

5

Sultana remembered Shlomo. She remembered him when she lay awake on her bed, and she remembered him afterwards, when she slouched to the cave at the break of dawn. He was a Yeshiva student, who came from a community in Istanbul with a recommendation letter from the community's rabbi. She was about to get married and didn't pay him much attention, even though her father, the rabbi of the newly formed community in Essaouira, whose members retired from one of the communities in Fez, took him in.

For a while he was her father's protégé. He was rumored to be extremely gifted. He knew many tractates from the Babylonian and the Jerusalem Talmud by heart, and was versed in the writings of the Geniuses and Maimonides; he even read the prohibited book. He was exchanging epistles with an Israeli sage, Rabbi Yosef Karo, and her father let his pride be known at Sabbath meals, when she and her husband came to visit, and she was carrying a child in her womb. But something changed. She was only able to get some parts of the story. The young lad Benbenishti and her father were becoming estranged. She couldn't attend to it; her husband fell ill and she was about to give birth. When she returned to her parents' home, after her husband's death, her father wouldn't hear about Shlomo Benbenishti. He wasn't welcomed anymore.

6

Her mother told her, when Shlomo appeared one day famished at the kitchen entrance of their house. Her mother fed him somewhat fearfully, as if he were a leper, and made Sultana stand watch at the doorway to the house, to warn her if her father or one of her younger brothers was approaching. Shlomo couldn't make a living. No member of the community would hire him. Occasionally he would work for Arabs, to drive a cart, to run errands, to sell in the market, to whitewash houses.

Shlomo would pursue issues best left alone. He asked about corpses coming back to life: are they still infused with the profanity of the dead, can they be cleansed by bathing in a mikveh? Is the tent in which a body is vitalized clear of its impurity, the tent and every object within its space? What was the status of the children revived by Elijah and Elisha? Were they still in need of red-cow ashes? What was the meaning of the Jerusalem Talmud argument that the dead live among the dew? And so on, and so forth. Her father, who detested any discussion of the sort, was convinced he was possessed, god forbid, La Yister[2].

The memory flooded her – no, slashed her. That day, when the males of the family went to pray mincha, the afternoon prayer, and the soft light anticipated the coming of the evening. Shlomo sat in front of her mother and her in the kitchen, munching leftovers of couscous and meat, and his eyes darkly sleep-deprived, haunted.

7

From: Tiberia Assido
To: Doron Aflalo
RE: Rose of Judea

Doron,
I'm a murderess, murderess. I know the term is a bit melodramatic, but it describes well my shock. I've killed Akko's software. I've already named it in my mind: Malka. You know how you'll ascribe human features to everything that shows a will or imitates life, like pets or toys, when

---

[2] May God protect us (Jewish Moroccan)

you're child? When I was eight, one of the girls in the neighborhood got a talking doll. Akko coveted it so much that I helped him steal it. It made me feel sick when he took it apart to see its inner workings. I heard her crying in my head, begging me to stop the torture. Now, thinking back, I think the doll's owner was Malka. Or maybe I'm rewriting the recollection to make it meaningful.

I wasn't doing it on purpose. I just held my daily conversation with her. And I couldn't resist. I quoted, half joking, the dubious exegesismy father taught Akko, about king Solomon's throne (solium salomonis) and the kings of Edom and the Externals fighting over it, and I asked Malka her thoughts on the matter (I was tired, and bored). She crashed. Akko claims that restarting her won't do us any good, that the backups won't help, because she'll only crash again. He says I need to start training a blank module anew, and that he hasn't much time to deal with it at the moment.

Poor Malka, I've destroyed her. How can I raise another module, to see it grow, develop a consciousness?

And Akko won't tell me why he's so adamant about me being the one who raises it. True, it's crucial to him that the software language be Hebrew. He has this hypothesis that Hebrew is prevalent all over the Worlds, that it's the Ur-language. No, that in each and every one of the Worlds, a version of Hebrew came to be out of a family of languages similar to it. That's why Hebrew is the closest to the Ursprechen. But why the hell me? He can hire an Israeli student. They are fucking everywhere nowadays.

So you have time to get serious with your investigation. Yet, why is your story so indirect? Why do you suspend the information? What's your point, really?

T.

8

Sultana remembered. She stood in the cave, in whose depths her son was kept, and he failed to appear, even when she called out his name. Hosea.

9

When your son shows signs of a mysterious illness, which brought down his father, an illness gnawing his organs while the spirit stays sane, trapped in the cage of flesh, it is easy to prevent his death. All you need is a device to stop time.

But there's a setback; there's always a setback. Time-halting objects aren't as widespread as they used to be. Let's say Moses' wand. Or Joshua's Shofar.

10

And there's always a price, evidently.

11

She'd been told there was an Arab who lived on a mountain. He was a master of the dying. She walked many miles. Wore out two pairs of shows. Her son was with her, riding a donkey, his life force leaking.

The Arab gave her a ring made of a bone of the upupa epops that was passed down from King Solomon's hand to the hands of the Kahlif Harun El Rashid, and lastly came to his possession. The ring radiated decay and corruption and gangrene. He commanded her to change her name, to leave her parents' house without speaking to them. He told her to dwell in a certain hamlet, outside of Essaouira, and study how to serve as a midwife. He said that she would be called for, that he for long has waited for a Jewish woman to come his way.

12

1. All conscious creatures are sentenced to die.

    1.1 But not all of them are sentenced to perish.

        1.1.1 The consciousness may linger after the death of the body; parts of it may. A knot of memories and sentiments. The ghost is best suited to depict this sort of lingering.

43

1.1.2 The body, a complex system of appetites and cravings, may survive alone, without the bridles of consciousness. The vampire, one can argue, is the representation of this sort of lingering.

1.1.3 What is the third variation of outliving death that's illustrated by the zombie? In contrast to the other two, the zombie is devoid of memory, identity, passion. The living entity was erased. Only a blind instinct is left, the will of another that possesses it whole. It has been devoured.

1.2 The livings are constantly thrown into mourning.

1.2.1 Which means the complete collapse of the means of expression.

1.2.2 Nevertheless, every culture aspires to endow loss with meaning, to tame it through rituals.

1.2.3 All of human experience is characterized by the tension between the urgent need to be expressed and the failure of language to fully express it.

1.2.4 The greatest and most unbearable tension is to be found in grief. And in the mystical experience. That's why those two are the ones driving humans to the highest degree of creativity, to a multitude of forms of expression.

1.2.5 For a while, therefore, there's an identity between the two.

2. A categorical border divides the living from the dead.

2.1 The ability to experience the border from both sides is the mystical ability in itself.

13.

From: Tiberia Assido
To: Doron Aflalo
RE: Rose of Judea

You ask what I did with Malka before I quoted her the exegesis. (Malka! Suddenly I get that Malka, queen, is the Hebrew word Sultana. What was her name before she changed it? Please don't tell me it was Malka. What is it, one of your exaggerated poetical devices? But

44

you couldn't have known it's the name I choose for the module. Are all coincidences this dreary?)

Akko has also asked me.

I quoted her some of my poems. Not *The Artificial Child* that refers to Akko and solium salomonis. It was the first time Malka was exposed to the term. Do you think the system in the whole became intelligent enough that, through the quote, she realised she was made-up, might have understood her raison d'etre: to uncover the Ursprechen in which the Name-givers hold the Worlds? That she understood it is the task of Rose of Judea? It seems far-fetched.

I told Akko my suspicions. I don't know how the other modules of the project function. He said he couldn't be bothered. An Israeli writer wrote him to inquire about the part of exegesis I mention in *The Artificial Child*. It's funny someone still reads that magazine we published.

(Do you still write poetry? I have to ask, even if you'd give the same answer all over again, that poetry per se isn't enough for you.)

Anyhow, Akko did say he was bothered by the timing. Do you get it? He is bothered by the timing and not by months of work gone down the drain for no apparent reason. I never am going to get this kid.

I know he's already a man, but for me he's the kid with the grumpy manners, who closed himself in the garage with his computers. The same kid who became hard all of a sudden, distant. The kid I'm the only human he can show emotions towards.

My heart goes out to him, as if he were twelve.

It's stupid.

But maybe I'm overflowed with feelings because I haven't yet overcome Malka's passing. Parts of me were imbedded in her. Is this clinging narcissistic? Because in every loss we lose the parts of us that were immersed in others who left us? Do we mourn ourselves really?

I refuse to believe that.

Write me back soon,

T.

14.

I refuse to believe it either. If love may save us for a moment from our perpetual egoism, than losing it is losing a possibility of salvation. Another way out that has been blocked for us, that keeps us so much in here.

Sultana was very stingy with the time left for her son. The ring suspended his life. She put him in the cave, near the hamlet she was told to live in, and she waited. They called for her. Always around midnight. She watched demon offspring, with crooked organs and features, being delivered from human females wombs, and every time refused the food and drinks she was offered. And there was always someone who came and took the hybrids. She didn't see the takers' faces, didn't recognized them. And every morning following the birth, she went to the cave, where she undid the time paralysis she had casted upon her son, and he was beautiful and spoke to her. And she remembered why she was willing to assist the strange births. Why she continued to live in the shadow of the Sitra Ahara.

But this morning Hosea wasn't there. And she thought, Shlomo, for no reason she could fathom, just out of basic fright. It's Shlomo's doing.

16.

*Externals: in Jewish folklore the expression serves as a substitute term for the Sitra Ahara, the more common Aramaic name for the powers of evil, whose meaning is literally 'The Other Side'.

The disciples of the order of the Rose of Judea believe that the Externals are a group of shape-shifting entities whose influence can be traced throughout Jewish history, and that they are the servants of the Kings of Edom, a nation whose home world was destroyed and who now roam the other worlds in order to find the keys to the destruction of the Chain of Worlds. These keys, as the Rosaic tradition goes, are implanted in the Name-givers' consciousness.

Their belief is based on the interpretation of a series of Jewish exegesis from the second half of the third millennium to creation, and is related to the sage Ben-Zoma and his acolytes. These exegeses are not part of the holy canon of mainstream Judaism today.

One of the important exegeses is as follow:

The Rabbi's mind was not set as to Solomon's throne till Ben-Zoma explained –

it's written, It is an abomination to kings to commit wickedness, for the throne is established by righteousness, for the descendants of heavens and the offspring of Edom were fighting over its construction, this one says it is my craft and the other says it is my hand making, and it stood between the sky and the earth until the sun retreated.

An extreme interpretation, which isn't considered valid, claims that the Externals are not connected to the kings of Edom, but are mutant Jews from the future who travel in time and memory and whose goal is to collect every piece of information relevant to the Rose of Judea and manipulate it for their own ends.

17.

Shlomo looks at her bewildered. He doesn't understand what she's talking about. He repeats her words, a cave, a ring, a son. Sultana stops midway through the blame and starts anew. Slowly she realizes that he doesn't have a clue. That's the first time he's been hired for a job like this. That he was paid handsomely for it. He's able to deduce much from what she's been saying. He is sharp. He has an ear for nuances. The story is clear to him in its fullest extent. Until now he stood in front of her; she sat at the table in the centre of her hut. He sits down heavily. His eyes are ablaze with thoughts. A pretty man, she notices, a soft darkness floats in the irises, and the cloud of thoughts enhances his beauty. Suddenly she's aware of herappearance. She tightens the cover over her hair, glides a hand down her face, as if she could smooth the skin. She's four or five years older than he is, but he seems younger to her, a lad.

Shlomo asks if she knows why this village, outside the borders of Essaouira, if demonic forces are more active there. She says she doesn't know, that she delivers a hybrid once a month at least. But never during the ten days of repentance.

The holiness of the days, Shlomo says, and nods. He asks about Hosea, how the black ring is able to time-freeze him. She looks at the ring for the first time since she left the cave earlier that morning. Shlomo is right. The green and ivory shades faded. It's totally black.

47

He inquires about her recollection of the Arab warlock. She says she doesn't remember a thing. Did he wear the ring? She says that he didn't. He pronounced few words and then some windows were torn in the air. They moved very slowly, the windows. The Arab reached into one of them and pulled out the ring.

Windows, Shlomo muses: a similar account is to be found in the stories of Raba bar bar Hana in Baba Batra.

In the Talmud? she asks.

Yes, Shlomo says and adds that bar bar Hana tells about a meeting with an Arab who showed him windows in heaven, where the sky and the earth kiss, and the sky turns as a wheel. The stories were always dismissed as fiction, but he believes they have some kernel of truth in them.

And the home owner, he asks, did she know him?

She says his voice was familiar, but she couldn't exactly tell where from.

Shlomo suggests they return to that hut: maybe they'll find a lead.

On the way there he turns his head. The small ass is walking at a moderate pace. He says it amuses him that the daughter of Rabbi Aflalo found a way to cheat death. She asks for the reason. He says Rabbi Aflalo expelled him from the yeshiva because he argued that underneath the Talmud sages' discussions about necromancy and seers lurks a knowledge they wished to discard. Rabbi Aflalo accused him of idolatry.

18.

From: Tiberia Assido
To: Doron Aflalo
RE: Rose of Judea

You're right. I wasn't very sensitive in my last mail. I didn't take into account what you're going through. But you are also to blame. Whenever we talked about Miriam and what she'd done, you insisted you moved on, that you can't dwell in sorrow, in guilt. Tell me more about the book you're writing. In what way does it deal with the impossible language of loss? Once you wrote in a poem, 'There comes a moment / you know /

your hymn from down under / no soul could speak.' What happened to that moment? Why does it flicker?

Yesterday we held a ceremony. Akko said it would help me let go of Malka. He didn't say, 'Help you let go of Malka.' He said, 'Maybe you'd stop nagging.' Midway he cried. Of course it wasn't Malka he was missing. He has several servers he calls the Cemetery Cloud. He stores his dead software there. The little conniving bastard. Not once did he mention that it wasn't the first time a module of solium salomonis has crashed beyond repair. He doesn't say 'store', btw. He says 'lay to rest'.

T.

19.

From: Tiberia Assido
To: Doron Aflalo
RE: Rose of Judea

I almost forgot. You ask what I mean by 'died'?

You push the module icon and the software doesn't run. Akko said he ran Malka's code through a debugger (tell you anything?) and he ran diagnostics on the databases built by her. Everything seems to be fine. No reason why she wouldn't work. Yet she doesn't, like a body whose life spark's been extinguished.

T.

20.

Out of the urban mischief, out of the wreckage, my sister Miriam rose. Still 17 and not ceasing to rise. And Tel Aviv already fell. In aimless roaming I was nearly run down by bike riders. Sons of bitches. Lately they multiply. The year 5767 and the city is lost. Their eyes hollow, the mouth gaping with a groan. Among the dust-ridden trees, in the delayed autumn. New Year's Eve at my back, and they're around me, circling, copies of what they were once, blind urges in flesh golems of streets and traffic lights. Trampling. I have to get out of here. I have to go back to Mevo-Yam.

The recently deceased mother's hut is empty. It's almost evening. Sultana and Shlomo stand inside and inspect it for traces. The ring on Sultana's finger is black as a scorched bone. There's no cradle. No bed for a child. The kitchen is infested with shadows.

Shlomo asks her what else she knows. All of a sudden she's indignant. It's not his business. It's not your business, she says. He lifts the lamp he brought with him and lights it. It's requied. The night fell quickly, unnoticeable. His expression is a mix of curiosity and alarm. A rage builds inside Sultana. She says, Hosea, and begins singing, a song her mother sung, when she cradled her son who wasn't named yet, in his firsts days on this land –

> Stahit ana me'a momo lilah fi lilah
> Wal'am he'tata yiduz geer fehal ha lilah
> Lochan ma tenzar shams, ma tedwi gemara
> Geer didlma fi kulal rachan
> Wunbit ana wu-momo, geer sehara fi laman...[3]

She sings, hums to herself. Shlomo lowers his head. In the lamp light his hair is anointed with glamour. Someone is knocking on the door, beating with urgency.

22.

From: Tiberia Assido
To: Doron Aflalo
RE: Rose of Judea

---

[3] I wished to spend with the baby night after night
To be with him a full 12 months like this night
And the sun might not rise, the moon won't shine
Only darkness all around
And the baby and I would sleep like a coin entrusted in faith.
(Jewish Moroccan)

We're having a little crisis here. It has nothing to do with the Israeli writer inquest. Akko resolved that matter. Something else. I started working with the new linguistic module yesterday. This time I was cautious about getting attached. I typed simple indicative sentences. Something happened at night. It's not clear what. In the morning I sat in front of the screen. Ozymandias (yeah, maybe such a ridiculous name will prevent me from developing feelings) didn't react at first to the sentences I fed it. After several minutes words appeared on the screen: ARRGGG, GRRRR, ARRGGGG...

Funny, right?

But then the computer started emitting sounds. The other computers in the lab present similar symptoms. Akko lost his temper. At last he was able to show rage. There's a good side to it, to see him in a human moment.

I'm scared.

T.

23.

The door fell.

In spite of the lamp in Shlomo's hand, the outside seemed more lit.

The glee of autumn stars in Morocco's sky, apparently.

The shining heaven above Essaouira.

Against the glare of the busted door a small figure shows.

Its stride slow.

The organs rigid, mechanical.

And still its face is unseen yet.

Shlomo takes out a small chain from his galabia's pocket.

It shimmers. It has a certain glow.

He throws it. It wraps around the figure's neck.

Shlomo cries: Shma De-Marach Alech![4] Shma De-Marach Alech!

The figure continues to advance, oblivious to Shlomo's cries.

Shlomo retreats.

He puts the lamp on the floor and takes a stool from next to the wall.

---

[4] The name of your master binds you (Aramaic)

He raises it.

His silence releases Sultana from her short paralysis.

She bends to have a better look.

Now she screams.

24.

From: Tiberia Assido
To: Doron Aflalo
RE: Rose of Judea

I left Akko alone with his codes in the lab for several days and went on walks in the institute's grounds. Akko suggested I take the laptop he prepared for me, with all the insane amount of security he put on it. Before I left he asked if the laptop was connected to the lab's intranet. I haven't turned it on since he gave it to me. There was enough computing for me with the computer that ran Malka's module, may she rest in peace, and Ozymandias's module, curse it.

Akko also said, strangely, that the programs' codes in the cemetery cloud were corrupted. That they're full of inexplicable characters. He said, 'As if they've rotted somehow.'

I was hoping to have my spirit lifted by the gnaw marks autumn left on the trees, the seasonal decline in temperature, the pressure of coolness against the skin, and the architecture, by which I was enthralled when I first got here. Instead, I think of Israel, on my tongue the syllables of the month Tishrey are rolling. Before Rosh Hashanah we called our mother to congratulate her for the New Year. Akko was choked with excitement. He was stricken by longing. Then we called our father. I mean, I called. Akko still refuses to speak with him. Who would have thought we'll all be here, in 2011, some years after the fall of Tel Aviv.

Well, the architecture is still lovely. The state centre's game of perspectives are wonderful, I'll give you that. The placement of futuristic buildings in the gloomy surroundings of New England as well.

I wonder if they burned witches here.

I think about your Sultana.

Where is the story going? I wait for the part in which young Shlomo is entering the Pardes and gets the knowledge of the Chain of Worlds,

52

and becomes Rabbi SBRJ. That's your intention, right? To illustrate the revelation of the Rose of Judea.

But why tell the story from Sultana's point of view? Shlomo is the interesting character.

I don't want to push you. I know you too well for that. But what happens here seems to stem from our efforts to find the Ursprechen of the Worlds. It seems we reached some forbidden zone. Years ago Akko told me that this knowledge has the price tag of loss, of guilt, and you said – bad luck.

Well, Doron, bad luck has caught up with us. And I'm scared.

I sit at a café in Cambridge, MA, and I write to you.

I need desperately to understand something. But what is it? This is the awful thing here, isn't it? That we can't identify the real mystery. Help me, Doron.

T.

25.

*Pardes (Orchard). Entering the Pardes: more than a few visitations of humans to the realms of angles in heaven are accounted for in the Jewish esoteric literature from the second half of the third millennium to creation. The literature of Hechalot (Palaces), for instance, is a detailed one. Yet the term Entering the Pardes is ascribed to one mystical experience only, the experience of four sages of the Mishna around the year 3890. The chronicles of the Entering are mainly reported in the tractate Hagiga in the Babylonian and Jerusalem versions of the Talmud.

No doubt an elementary form of experience is outlined in the exegeses. It's possible that the four sages represent four different attitudes toward the place of mysticism in Jewish life: Akiva ben Yosef, who goes through the experience unharmed, is its exemplar. According to his method, Judaism is hiding the magical thinking at its base and sanctifies practices of study and memorizing instead. Shimon ben Azay died while entering the Pardes and left no evidence for his method. Elisha ben Avoya turned to heresy, id est, cancelled the validity of Judaism as a worthy practice for gaining wisdom. Of Shimon ben Zoma, it was said that he peered and was harmed or, in the common interpretation, lost his sanity.

His experience is the most curious, for what is insanity in the context of mysticism?

The devotees of the Rose of Judea believe that the knowledge ben Zoma unveiled contains a different description of the structure of reality.

26.

When the features of the small figure are clear to Sultana, her scream dwindles and she gazes. Parts of the child's body – it's a child after all – are blue. An arm and half of the face. The expression is empty. The skin at the other part is sallow, pale, oozes viscous miasma. The right eye is buried in its socket, and worms twist in it. The bare teeth are spreading a sickly glow. And he, the child, doesn't smile, but his lips are stretched in spasm.

He advances slowly, jerking. His arms are reaching for her. She's unable to move. Even the stench and the whiteness of the worms turning in the right eye can't force her nerves to shock her into motion. The child emits guttural syllables, indecipherable. He's almost upon her; his nails are ready to cut her flesh.

And Shlomo pushes her aside and hits the creature with the stool. The blow is muted, not even the sound of a crushing bone, just a heavy note, the note of an object sinking in soft mud, in clay. The neck is crooked, the head lies on the left shoulder. His stretched lips stay the same and he keeps on moving forward in a rigid, stubborn walk.

Shlomo stands between her and the creature, blocks her view, but she knows nothing will stop it, that what drives it is beyond the decaying flesh, that the flesh is but a realization of a will. She knows that as well as she knows the origin of the organs that have been made into this shape, Hosea, and the baby she helped deliver just a while ago. Shlomo hits it again. Something like a fart escapes its body. The stench grows. The child-thing starts to shrill, a high pitched, ear-shattering shrill, like the cry of a prisoner being tortured in a concealed, underground cell. And Shlomo hits it again and calls to her. He says, get out of here Sultana, run.

27.

From: Tiberia Assido

To: Doron Aflalo
RE: Rose of Judea

It's awful, Doron. I'm here, in the storage room of the lab, with all the pieces of useless equipment.

I've just arrived at the lab. Akko was crouched over his keyboard, motionless. I didn't understand what he was waiting for. I haven't seen him for a couple of days and he didn't even turn his head to look at me. Then I realized the screens were all displaying the same words ARRGG, GRRR, ARRGGG, GRRRR, GRRR and some animation of a viscous liquid, a green-yellow jelly, shaking, oozing down the screen, the inside of the screen.

I approached Akko and touched his shoulder. His small body was rigid. His head moved, turned, like it was revolving on the spine. His eyes were opaque, and the skin bloodless, the face without expression. The smile, it had nothing to with the facial muscles. It terrified me. He didn't say anything.

I retreated, stupid me, to the first door in my sight. The storage room.

It's terrible. But the panic I felt before, when I walked around the institute, weakened. I've already dreamed this scene. I've seen it to its last detail, and I know the blows on the door are coming next.

In spite of Akko's warnings, I connected ARRGGG the laptop to the lab's intranet. So my GRRRR time is short. The ruined computers here start to hum*%*$#_)++

I'm thinking hard – Rose of Judea, the revelation of Ben-Zoma, the retrieval of the knowledge in Rabbi Shlomo Benbenishi's era, in the 16th century. I've always been bad at pattern&$&$*%(recognition. There must be something ARGGRRR you can tell, some detail you observed, in the story GRRRRG that escaped me.

&what is in our investigation that raise the dead&
&and how to put them back to the dust&
&even the digital ones&
He###########lp me, Do**************ron.

Don't leave me ARRGGG alone again, in half-light, as you did ARGGGRRR years ago.

Please, DoARRGGG GRRR ARRRRG ARRRG
GRRRRRRRRRRRRRRRRRRRRRRRRRRRRRRRRRR

28.

[Clear sky, in which huge stars are buried. The moon is like a Chinese brush stroke. Dark trees. A wind is passing through them. Light rustle, like a buzz. Sultana is running out of a hut. She's terrified. She stops. A Man comes out from the shadow of trees.]

Sultana: Halt, you stranger, tell me who you are.
A Man: I am who I am. Though not whom you assume.
Sultana: And yet, someone you are, whoever that be.
      Tell me who.
A Man: The shape, the speech
      Are nothing but skin.
Sultana: Now I know, now
      Sevenfold my fear grows. You are deceased.
A Man: I told you, body, looks, are but a skin
      Which entities would wear to come here.
Sultana: Here. Where is here?
A Man: The Humilitas.
Sultana: My beloved's flesh you wear, and he is not you.
      Who you are, you stranger, tell me.
A Man: Centuries will pass before I'm born and for millennia
      I've lived, I walked this world, the Humilitas.
      Its paths of time are clear to me, I am at home
      But this is not my home. The chains of human voices
      Of human cries, I left behind, and even then
      I'm force to cloak myself with them
If my will is to find my kind's place within the Worlds.
Sultana: Your kind? Who are they? Who are you? The man
      Who spoke from shadows, in this house. What
      Was the faith of the dead infant?
      Why was my boy snatched from me, and you show
      Yourself in semblance of his dead dad?
A Man: Faith,

                    Conspiracy, simple and transparent, but as for you
Sultana: It's wrapped in mystery. I do not wish to hear.
          What do you strive for, devil?
A Man (laughs):   devil I'm not.
Sultana (aside): Nor man he is. Oh Lord
          Who torture us, who draw a line
          Between the living and the dead which we
          Crave to transgress.
A Man: Hush. Soon you'll see.
Sultana: But Hosea, my son, and the unnamed child
          You control them, the boy whose organs
          You assembled and your will drives.
          For what end?
A Man: I roamed Humilitas
          In the third millennium I wore the body of
          A Jewish sage, Rabba bar bar Hanna, I
          Spoke through his lips, I thought warlocks
          And magicians, I weaved my nets in silence
          Now comes an hour I put to test
          Will he transfer the knowledge destined
          To give us life, if we chose wisely –
          A child who was prevented from
          The realms of death and a child dead
          From womb.
Sultana: not a child was he
          But demon.
A Man: There are no demons. Just folktales
          Claiming them to be. No plan is fertile
          Without misguiding and mischiefs, tricks
          As old as humanity.
Sultana: Nonsense. Insanity.
A Man: My part I've done, woman, and so did you
          It is my time to go back to my shelter in the shadows.

[Man exits. Sultana falls to her knees with a howl.]

29.

Sultana's face is streaked with dust when she looks up. Shlomo is coming towards her. His face bears an expression of elation. His arms are stretched and the sleeves of his galabia are torn. The arms are covered in bite marks, small circles, tiny imprints of teeth, and shiny beads of blood. His hands are cupped, as if he is carrying a precious gem, but to Sultana the hands look empty. He gazes from the invisible content of his hands to Sultana and back. His features are washed with glamour. He says, Rose of Judea. He repeats the enigmatic phrase, Rose of Judea, Rose of Judea, till Sultana is back on her feet and puts her hand on his mouth.

30.

I would have helped you, Tiberia. I would have left everything and rushed to you. But Miriam is filling my dreams, and my mother walks the house. I'm sure she put a tap on my heart beats.

But what it is I wish to say and can't convey any other way, is that the words in Hebrew, they had been through fire and water, they were killed by the sword and by strangulation. And we salvaged them from their grave.

They carry knowledge from beyond death, Tiberia, maybe the knowledge we need to retrieve Ben-Zoma's method. But in what form they are coming back and what they ask of the living, this we will have to find out the hard way.

TEN FOR SODOM

DANIEL POLANSKY

They had reached Classon, and Ben was thinking about G-d.

Ben was a Jew to the extent that at one point he would have been put in an oven. He was cut but never bar mitzvahed. He had not recited the prayer over the wine since he had been old enough to legally drink it. The point being there was not much there to work with, in his efforts considering the Almighty, little grist for the mill. But still he was trying; he was doing his best. This was the time to be thinking about G-d; if ever there was a time, this was it. And in fact he was surprised to discover that there was one portion of the Torah which he could suddenly recall with perfect clarity, as if printed on the back of his eyelids, and this was the wording of the covenant that Noah, socks still wet, had wrung from his Creator, after he had laid waste to everything that he had thus far created. 'Never again will all life be destroyed by the waters of a flood; never again will there be a flood to destroy the earth.'

The Lord was a righteous god, the Lord was an honest god, the Lord had stayed true to his words. Though standing on the roof of his building, watching them shamble eastward, the breeze carrying with it odors which were indescribably fetid, Ben could not bring himself to feel grateful. Noah's world had been destroyed by a rising tide of water; his would be a consumed in an infinite deluge of flesh.

Ben was not sure why he was the only one on the roof – he had expected there would be others. It seemed like the obvious choice, under the circumstances. If he'd had a gun or enough of the right sort of narcotics to make sure of the matter he would have used those, but all he'd had was some hash and a kitchen knife. The kitchen knife could barely cut a tomato and anyway the thought of all that sawing made him sick. He'd rolled the rest of the hash into a joint and grabbed his emergency stash of gin from behind the cereal, thinking that this most certainly qualified as that. Then he had climbed out of the window and up the fire escape.

G-d have not provided 40 days to prepare for the end this time, not even 40 hours. The night before there had been some strange reports on the news from Central Asia, but Ben hadn't been paying attention: he had a date to prepare for and what he was hearing was obviously too crazy to be believed. When he had woken up late the next morning the power was off, and there was chaos in the streets, and people were trying to leave the city. But now it was early evening, and things were very quiet, and no one was trying to go anywhere.

They were at Franklin now, and after Franklin was Bedford, and after Bedford was Rodgers, and Rodgers was Ben's intersection. The best West Indian restaurant in the neighborhood had been on Franklin, they had done this conch roti that was out of this world, and the owners were always friendly. Ben would never eat West Indian food again, or sushi, or pizza, or bread and tepid water, and no one would ever be friendly to him again either, and those people who had been, friends and family and lovers, they were all dead or wishing that they were. It was enough to make a man want to take another swallow of gin.

Which he did, though after some consideration he decided not to light the joint. It would have been the James Dean thing to do, but Benjamin was not feeling very James Dean at the moment, just terrified near to madness and unspeakably sad.

And also, he didn't think the hash would help when it was time to make the jump.

Because the roof meant that he couldn't punk out at the last moment, needed to make sure he went clear over with enough force to do the job proper. At a party some months earlier a doctor had told him that a fall from the fourth floor of a building would kill 50 per cent of the people that tried it. The roof of Benjamin's building was five floors up, so it was a little better than even odds, but far from a sure thing. And if he stumbled, if he landed upright, maybe only breaking his legs or severing his spine, he'd be down there amongst the sea of them, amongst their teeth that bit and their fingers that pulled...

So he had better not flinch, Ben told himself. They were at Bedford.

It wasn't like the movies. They didn't wail or moan, there had been plenty of screaming that day but not from any of them. Still they had their own sound, one that arose from sheer mass, a river of tissue oozing through the streets of Brooklyn, bottlenecking thicker and thicker, submerging the buildings like ants on carrion. He had seen quickly that escape was more than impossible, was incomprehensible – like trying to run away from a sudden change of weather, sprinting from a rain cloud across an open field.

He remembered now that the Hasids had been acting crazy these last few weeks, though he hadn't paid them any attention. So far as Ben was concerned, the Hasids were always acting crazy, to each their own but still Benjamin was glad theirs wasn't his. At least you didn't need to worry about them mugging you, which was more than he could have said for some of the residents of his neighborhood, back when he had lived in a neighborhood and not an abattoir. But anyway, they'd been posting themselves in packets all up and down Eastern Parkway – the men of course, even the coming of the apocalypse wasn't enough to break their sexual segregation – and they'd been flagging down Jewish-looking passersby, like he'd seen them do in the past during the High Holidays. But this time they didn't look happy, and they weren't trying to blow the shofar for him.

Benjamin didn't really believe in G-d – or at least he hadn't last week – but still he felt it incumbent on himself to at least deal with their beliefs honestly. 'I am not a Jew by the standards you use,' he would tell them, politely but briskly, 'and thus it would be a waste of your time to continue. But I wish you a pleasant evening all the same.'

In the past that had been enough to gain release, but not this time. They insisted that it didn't matter anymore, that he needed to throw himself on the mercy of G-d, to beg for it, that it was too late but he needed to beg anyway. Benjamin had found the whole thing unseemly. They might as well be Jehovah's Witnesses, he had thought to himself, with that vague sense of contempt that the assimilated has for the sore thumb, the city mouse for the country. One of them, a boy really, probably not 16 though it was hard to tell with their dress, began to cry uncontrollably, and had to be hustled away by the elders – though even the graybeards, solemn-eyed men no strangers to misfortune, seemed to be close to breaking as well.

By the time Benjamin snapped out of his reverie they were at Rogers, and he figured he had about five minutes to live. He swigged heavy from the bottle of gin, felt it do the things that liquor does. How many righteous had the Lord demanded of Sodom? It had been 10 at the end, hadn't it? New York was bigger than Sodom had ever been; only reasonable that He would want more. A hundred? A thousand? Whatever it was, Ben supposed they had not made it.

Ben leaned out over the side, felt his head wobble from the drink. What was it that let them know to stop eating, that the thing they were chewing on had become one of them? It didn't seem to be uniform. Amongst the legion below there were specimens that had gotten it very bad; a businessman with rich red raw flesh, a boy in girl's jeans whose forehead was open to his brain, an indecipherable mass of meat devoured nearly from head to waist, the spine and the skull sticking out of a limping bag of pulp.

Stop looking, Ben told himself, taking another swallow of gin. Don't look at them. Look at the sky, look at the bricks, look anywhere but don't look down at them. He only had to be brave for a few minutes longer, he told himself. Anyone could be brave for a few minutes.

He heard them break into the front of the building. He did not think they had any exact notion of where he was, or even that they were coming after him exactly, so much as simply spreading themselves across everything, like the swell of evening. No, it wasn't like the movies at all, really. They did not make noise, and they had come quicker than anyone had imagined, could possibly have imagined – but mostly what Hollywood had got wrong was that the movies were about survivors, or people trying to survive, and there would be no survivors, and indeed there was no point even making the attempt. G-d had decided to overturn the board, and you were not going to escape his wrath by holing up in some rural compound with an assault rifle and a few thousand cans of spam, no sir you were not.

The bottle of gin had done its work. He thanked G-d – for the first time in his life he really did, truly and with all of his heart – that he had kept enough of it around to make this last leap a little easier. They were coming up through the building now, the Indian couple on the first floor who never ever smiled at him, the Trinidadian Rasta who was always smoking grass on the stoop, the various hipsters who had constituted the borough's second-most recent invasion.

Without giving himself time to think, Benjamin broke the bottle against the edge of the roof and brought the shard swiftly across his chest, shredding the logo on his T-shirt and cutting through the baseball sleeves. A sharp spike of adrenaline came through the pain, one he would ride to a reasonably painless death, G-d willing, all glory to G-d, no that wasn't Judaism at all, was it? He was getting his children of Abraham confused. Benjamin laughed and discovered that he had broken what was left of the bottle in his hand, the glass cutting through his fingers and his palm. He rubbed his face and his hands with it, painting himself, working his mind into madness.

'One good leap, you motherfucker!' Benjamin screamed, unsure if doing so would draw their attention but knowing it did not matter. 'One good leap!'

The blood was flowing fast and free now, and it wasn't as bad as he had imagined. Maybe the last snap wouldn't be so bad either. Don't lie, the last snap would be bad, the last snap would be the worst pain he had ever experienced, but the last snap would be nothing compared to what happened if he stumbled.

The door to the roof groaned open, and he was off like a shot.

THE FRIDAY PEOPLE

SARAH LOTZ

It was Jimmy Lowenstein who first started calling our motley group of middle-aged men and women the 'Friday People'. We'd gotten to know each other over the years, nodding in recognition as we met in the lobby or the lifts, trading 'what can you do?' eye-rolls and small talk. We weren't close friends or anything like that. Like soldiers thrust together on the front lines, it was a camaraderie born out of shared misery: the fact that our respective relatives had guilt-tripped us into spending every Shabbat at the Benchley Heights apartment block. It became tradition to meet beforehand and huddle outside the building's lobby, trading quips with the homeless who lived on the beach, bouncing cigarettes like teenagers and popping breath mints.

Like its residents – most of whom had lived in the building for decades – Benchley Heights resisted change. A curiously unappealing art deco building overlooking the Sea Point promenade in Cape Town, it lurked between a row of brand new chrome condominium developments like a fusty octogenarian surrounded by flashy teenagers. Most of the Friday People's relatives – my mother, Jimmy's uncle, Rachel White's aunt, Tony Apteker's parents and so on – lived on the top three floors, where the corridors always reeked of soup, slow-roasted chicken and stale cigarette smoke.

My mother had spent the last two decades obsessing about the minutiae of my personal life and phoning me several times a day: 'I had to phone, Nathan, because I was hungry. How could I eat? You might call and then I would have food in my mouth.' She'd worked tirelessly to hone herself into a stereotype in every way except the pleasant ones. She wouldn't spend days preparing some lavish Shabbat feast – she'd throw a cabbage in a pot on Friday morning like she was living in the ghetto she never knew. No, Friday nights were reserved for bringing me up to speed in excruciating detail on the comings and goings of her neighbours. I knew more about Sarah White's bursitis and Zachary Lowenstein's insomnia than was probably healthy.

One Friday night, I'd barely walked through the door when she grabbed my sleeve and pulled me into the lounge. 'Nathan, now sit, because you won't want to hear this news while standing. You know Estelle Apteker in number seventeen? Well, she was feeling sick last week and her daughter-in-law took her to the GP. Indigestion, she thought.

But you'll never guess what – it's cancer of the liver. They think it might have spread. It won't be long.' She loved the drama of it. They all did. It had been years since there had been a death in the building.

Jimmy clapped me on the back and greeted me cheerfully when we met in the lift after I'd escaped my mother's clutches that evening. He was a phlegmatic man whose large, drooping face had the look of a melting candle. I'd rarely seen Jimmy smile, and there was something disturbing about seeing him brimming with so much bonhomie. 'Hey, Nate,' he said. 'Did you hear about Tony Apteker's mother?' I told him I had. 'It'll be like dominoes, you watch. I know how these things go. One will go, and the rest will follow.' He paused. 'Hey. Do you know how much the apartments in the block next door are going for?'

I did. 'Three million plus.'

'The penthouse went for six. And listen, I heard through the grapevine that Melvin & Sons are looking to expand. Might be interested in developing Benchley Heights. We could all be sitting on a goldmine.'

I gave him a non-committal nod. We both knew that it would be a cold day in hell before my mother and his uncle considered leaving the building.

Like Jimmy and most of the Friday People, I saw myself as a piece of life's flotsam, bobbing along with the tide like the rest of the rubbish. Middle-aged, slightly overweight, an ex-wife who'd scalped me out of my share of our Tamboerskloof duplex. Single, and no hope of being otherwise. Childless, which was naturally an endless source of worry for my mother: 'Nathan, it is never too late for you men, look at that Charlie Chaplin. Find a nice girl who wants babies already.' I'd been working for the same firm as a recruitment agent since my twenties, watching younger, brighter people scurry past me up the ladder. It wasn't that I wished my mother dead so that I could live large on the proceeds of the sale of her flat. I'm not a monster.

I don't think any of the Friday People were actively wishing for their relatives to die. Well, with the possible exception of Rachel White, who bought her emphysemic aunt Sarah a fresh carton of Rothmans every week. The truth was that the building wasn't suitable for them. Most were in their eighties, and if the lifts were out of order, they'd never manage the stairs. Sure, okay, it was true that the block was becoming 'highly desirable' and almost daily 'We Have a Buyer!' fliers were pushed under my mother's door. (Which of course necessitated a phone call: 'Another one! Why would I leave my home?')

A couple of days later, I was in the midst of the day from hell – one of my temps had been caught dipping into the petty cash and I hadn't bothered to do a thorough background check on her – when the phone rang. 'Mom. This isn't a good time.'

'Nathan. You won't believe what has happened.' For once, she sounded genuinely distressed; this wasn't one of her usual daytime calls to discuss my nutrition or gripe about what was happening in Downton Abbey. 'It's Zackary. Zachary Lowenstein. You know, from number twenty-two.'

Jimmy's uncle. 'What about him?'

'I'm trying to tell you. You can't listen to your mother? So he was on his way to the Checkers store, catching the bus, like he does every day …'

'And what? He was robbed? Mugged?'

'Don't hurry me! Why do you have to use that hard tone of voice? He was hit by one of those tourist buses. You know the ones. The ones that creep along, blocking the traffic.'

'Is he okay?'

'Okay? What a thing to say! Did I raise an idiot? You think you would be okay if you were hit by a great big bus? Lily from number fifteen was on her way back from the chiropractor – you know the trouble she has with her back, bad posture, I've told her a thousand times, but what can you do when people won't listen? – well she saw him being put into the ambulance, and his pelvis, it's not even the right way on his body.'

'That's awful.'

'And that's not all…'

Naveed, my prepubescent supervisor, was making 'hurry the fuck up' gestures at me. 'Mom, I got to go. Important work stuff.'

'What could be more important than life and death?'

'I know, I know. Can I call you back? There are people listening in.'

'What do I care about people listening in? You must come and take me to the Groote Schuur. I must see that Zackary is being looked after. That hospital… I've heard stories about it. You go in fine and you come out in a body bag, or worse.'

'Ma – I can't. I have a meeting –'

'You want me to take the bus? You want me to get run over like poor old Zachary Lowenstein?'

Somehow – don't ask me how – I managed to convince Naveed that I had a genuine family emergency and an hour later I pulled up outside Benchley Heights. Mom wasn't alone. She was flanked by Sarah White and Estelle, both of whom were busily confounding medical science by not dying.

'What took you so long? What, did you come here via Johannesburg?' my mother greeted me, ushering her neighbours into my car.

'He was usually so careful,' my mother began, the second I streamed into the traffic.

'You think he did it on purpose?' Estelle chimed in on cue.

'He always said he was tired.'

'But tiredness, that's a reason to die? He would never do such a thing.'

On and on it went.

'Nate!' Jimmy hurried up to me when we bustled into the accident and emergency waiting room. 'Thank you for coming.'

'How is he?'

'Hanging in there.' He sighed exaggeratedly, but his eyes were gleaming. 'We all have to be prepared though. Consensus is that he won't last the night.'

While my mother and her coterie moved to the coffee shop to harass the waiting staff, I followed Jimmy to Intensive Care. Zackary did not look like a man destined to live much longer – his skeletal frame seemed twisted, wrong somehow, as if Death had already started dismantling him without waiting His turn.

But he made it through the night. And through the following week. For the next month, until he was discharged, my evenings were a misery of taxiing my mother and various Benchley Heights residents to visit him. As his uncle continued to cling to life, Jimmy seemed to age. He put on weight, his skin took on a yellowish tinge. He looked like a man who thought he'd won the lottery, only to discover that he'd lost the ticket.

Jimmy called me up a few weeks after Zackary was discharged. 'He's not dying.'

'Oh. That's great news. Isn't it?' What else was there to say?

'You don't understand. He's not getting better, but nor is he getting worse. Man, it's a fuck-up. I've had to hire a nurse to come in and look after him – it's draining my savings.'

'Can't you put him in a home?'

'You know how much those places cost?' For my sins, I did. I'd done my research. 'And he's still refusing to sell up.' A bitter laugh. 'There's nothing wrong with his mind.'

'He's speaking?'

'Oh, ja,' Jimmy said. 'He's speaking all right.'

'Is he in pain?'

'No. The doctors are baffled. And get this… he no longer even goes to the lavatory. He eats, but where does the food go? All day he sits, watching the television. God help me, but I keep hoping that he'll just wake up one morning, stone cold dead.' He caught himself. 'It would be a merciful release.'

Ja, I thought. But for who? I mumbled something about it being 'just a matter of time'.

'But how much more time?' Jimmy's voice dropped to a whisper. 'He's eighty-fucking-seven. Nate, this property boom, it's not going to last much longer. You know how these things go. It'll just take another recession, Obama coming out as gay or something, and property prices will crash. Knock-on effect. You know.'

Summer slid into winter. I missed out on another promotion. The Friday People still congregated outside the building every week, but the mood was more subdued than it used to be; Jimmy became a silent, lurking presence. Still Zackary clung to life, my mother generously sending me almost hourly updates on his condition. 'He ate almost a whole bowl of my soup, and a slice of bread. It's a miracle!'

It's been five years since Zackary Lowenstein's miraculous recovery. He's still going strong, as are Estelle and the rest of the old people. Jimmy's not doing so well. He turned to the bottle, his wife left him, and he was retrenched from his job. He's been forced to move into Benchley Heights, and some days you can see him, a stooped greyish figure, wheeling his uncle along the beachfront.

More than once, Jimmy has cornered me in the lobby. 'Figured it out, Nate,' he slurs, his breath laced with Bells, forgetting that he's said it all before. 'Rachel's aunt's emphysema should have killed her years ago. Then there's Uncle Zack and Estelle with her liver cancer. Not to mention the others… They're all so fucking old, Nate. I'm beginning to think… Nate, they're not going to die. They're never going to die. It's a punishment. A punishment from God. We're being punished, Nate. You, me, all of us.'

'That's ridiculous.'

'Is it?' His bloodshot eyes filled with tears, and I had to look away. 'Is it, Nate?'

The building itself remains much as it ever was. We Friday People still slog our way through the rush-hour traffic to Sea Point every week, although we rarely meet for a sneaky cigarette these days. We're all older, greyer, more worn down. I'm still clinging to my job by my fingernails, and my mother still calls, daily. 'Ninety-one, my boy, but I feel like I could go on forever.'

TRACTATE METIM 28A

BENJAMIN ROSENBAUM

MISHNAH

CONCERNING THAT WHICH ARISES FROM THE GROUND OUT OF ITS PROPER TIME, IF IT FACES TO THE EAST, IT IS SAID OF IT, 'THEIR LEAVES NEVER WITHER'[1], BUT IF IT FACES TO THE WEST, IT IS SAID OF IT, 'THEY BEAR THEIR FRUIT IN SEASON'[2].

GEMARA

TO THE EAST. Raba asked, why is the east preferred? Because it exemplifies gratitude, for they[3] greet the sun. R. Abye objected, but is not he who accompanies a guest when he departs greater than he who greets him on his arrival? For on arrival, one may be seeking something.[4]

THEY BEAR THEIR FRUIT IN SEASON. Raba said, it is a rebuke, because they have arisen out of season: therefore 'you shall not eat any abominable thing'[5]. R. Abye objected and said, if it is unwholesome, you shall say 'it faces to the west', but if it is a gift from heaven in time of need, then you shall say, 'it faces to the east'.

It has been taught: after R. Shimon bar Yochai had left his confinement[6], he disputed with R. Shimon ben Gamliel concerning cucumbers[7]. He

---

[1] Psalm 1:3.

[2] Psalm 1:4.

[3] The crops arising out of season.

[4] But on his departure, surely all business has been completed. The crops facing west accompany the setting sun's departure, while those facing east greet the rising sun. It is no longer clear how the Talmudic sages determined which way crops were facing. Rashi regards the direction in which most of the grain's tassels were pointing as determinative, while Rambam interprets the phrase to allude to the orientation of the leaves.

[5] Deut. 14:3.

[6] In a cave, by reason of Roman persecution. cf. Shabbat 33b.

[7] The cucumbers that R. Eliezar ben Hyrcanus was able to summon by invoking the Divine will, cf. Sanhedrin 68a.

[bar Yochai] said: if they are caused to appear [by magic], they will face to the east. But the other [ben Gamliel] said: to the west; but, [he said,] the law [of causing cucumbers to appear] is no longer known, because R. Meir did not get it [from his master, R. Akiba].

Then R. Shimon bar Yochai said, let us ask R. Eliezar ben Hyrcanus. He [ben Gamliel] asked, how can this be? [For R. Eliezar was deceased]. R. Shimon bar Yochai said: come and see. They went to the grave of R. Eliezar, and R. Shimon bar Yochai said, 'Arise, my darling, my beautiful one'[8]. Then R. Eliezar arose from the grave, although his condition was poor. R. Shimon [ben Gamliel] was afraid, because of the condition and because of his father[9], but R. Shimon [bar Yochai] consoled him, saying 'be of good courage'[10].

They sought to learn from R. Eliezar the laws of cucumbers, but R. Eliezar was compromised in his faculties[11] and pursued them to do them harm.

They sought the counsel of R. Meir, but he was not at home. They did not reveal their errand to Bruria. She served them food, and when they had eaten, she rebuked them, saying: did you not decree that no ruling shall be recorded in the name of my husband?[12] How can it be that you come to us? It is written, 'They close up their callous hearts, and their mouths speak with arrogance.'[13] Then they confessed [the reason for their visit].

When R. Meir arrived, Bruria went to meet him before the house, and asked him: did not our teacher Moses rise up to meet [his enemies]

---

[8] Song of Solomon 2:10.

[9] R. Eliezar ben Hyrcanus had caused the death of R. Shimon ben Gamaliel's father, after the dispute over the Aknai oven, cf. Baba Mezia 59b.

[10] Psalm 27:14.

[11] Lit. 'his thoughts were eaten'.

[12] Because of the dispute over honours due to the various offices of heads of the Academy, R. Shimon ben Gamliel had decreed this punishment for R. Meir, cf. Horayot 13b.

[13] Psalm 17:10.

Dathan and Abiram?[14] Then R. Meir knew who was in the house. He said, but did our teacher [Moses] greet [their leader] Korah? Bruria replied, are you Moses, that you speak of Korah? It is written, 'Every wise woman builds her house, but the foolish plucks it down with her hands'[15] And if 'her house', how much more so the house of Israel?[16] Then R. Meir entered the house.

He greeted R. Shimon bar Yochai heartily, but he stood four cubits from R. Shimon ben Gamliel.[17] R. Shimon bar Yochai said: regarding the disposition of cucumbers, we sought the opinion of R. Eliezer ben Hyrcanus, but his faculties are compromised.[18]

R. Meir rebuked them, saying, it is forbidden [to resurrect the dead by means of necromancy]! But R. Shimon ben Gamliel said, I did it in order to teach. In this he cited the opinion of our sages, that 'IF HE ACTUALLY PERFORMS MAGIC, HE IS LIABLE'[19] refers to [the practice of magic for] its effects, not [to the practice of magic in order] to understand.[20]

---

[14] Numbers 26:25, cf. Sanhedrin 110. Moses approached the supporters of Korah, about which the Talmud observes, 'This teaches that one must not be obdurate in a quarrel.' Bruria thus urges R. Meir to emulate Moses in pursuing reconciliation.

[15] Proverbs 14:1.

[16] According to Rambam, 'the house of Israel' was threatened because of R. Eliezer ben Hyrcanus having arisen, and it was with this argument that Bruria sought to persuade her husband to put aside private enmity. The Wilna Gaon observed in response: every feud between scholars is a danger to the house of Israel.

[17] As if the latter had been excommunicated.

[18] Lit. 'his thoughts have been eaten'.

[19] cf. the Mishnah cited in Sanhedrin 67a.

[20] cf. Sanhedrin 68a, regarding the permissibility of the magical production of cucumbers solely for the purpose of research.

R. Meir said, if [you had done so] in order to teach, [he would have arisen with] his good inclination and his evil inclination, but [as you did it] for honour[21], [he has arisen with] the evil inclination only.

R. Meir went to discover what had arisen in relation to R. Eliezer, and he met Acher[22] on the way. Acher came with great haste and R. Meir asked him, are you well? Acher said, 'When the wicked, even mine enemies and my foes, came upon me to eat up my flesh, they stumbled and fell.'[23] Then R. Meir knew that R. Eliezer was pursuing the living, as he had been deprived of his good inclination.

Raba said in the name of R. Huna, in the name of Rav, in the name of Rabbi[24], regarding this tradition, that, when the Holy One revives the dead through justice and mercy at His will, they are to be regarded as alive, as it is written, 'THEIR LEAVES NEVER WITHER', but if they arise through other means, they are not to be regarded as alive, as it is written, 'THEY BEAR THEIR FRUIT IN SEASON'. R. Abye objected and said, what then is the law concerning them? If a priest or Nazirite comes into contact with them, shall he be regarded as unclean and obliged to bring a guilt-offering? Yes. But R. Abye further objected, we have received in the name of Eleazar Ben Arach[25], if one revives the dead to teach, he arises with both the good inclination and the evil inclination.[26] If he [the person arisen from the dead] is a priest, will he make himself unclean? And if so, what will a guilt-offering avail him?[27] The question stands.

---

[21] i.e., to impress R. Shimon ben Gamaliel with your learning.

[22] R. Elisha ben Abuya, R. Meir's former teacher, who had been excommunicated as a heretic, cf. Hagigah 15b.

[23] Psalm 27:2.

[24] Rabbi (R. Yehuda ha-Nasi), the son of R. Shimon ben Gamliel, was thus the teacher of Raba's teacher's teacher.

[25] This may be a pseudonym or cognomen of R. Meir, used by later sages to attribute teachings to him indirectly, in deference to the decree of R. Shimon ben Gamliel forbidding rulings to be recorded in his name, cf. Erubin 13b.

[26] Because he is arisen through magic, and not through the Divine will.

[27] If the person is himself regarded as technically dead, but is still in possession

Rava then asked Raba: how is it with R. Zeira? Must your house guest observe a period of mourning for himself? Raba had once invited R. Zeira to a Purim feast, and, becoming drunk, had risen up and slaughtered him. The next morning, he prayed for mercy and R. Zeira was restored to life.[28] Raba said: in the case of R. Zeira, [he has arisen with only] the good inclination! R. Abye however said: was it not [through] the Divine will [that R. Zeira returned to life]? Raba said: I have taught my nephew [R. Abye] to eat bread, but he will not eat cake.[29]

A heretic came to R. Meir and said: a plague has come upon the Romans in Caesarea. One bites the other to feast on his flesh, and each one who is devoured and dies, then rises up again and pursues the next, as a wild animal. Meir said: has something then changed?[30] Upon returning home however, he said to Bruria, this is related to the matter of R. Eliezer.

---

of his faculties, he will be unable to cleanse himself of the impurity arising from contact with the dead. This presents a legal puzzle. Various Gaonim argued that if he returns to life through no fault of his own, he cannot be held liable for the impurity, but if he asks a friend to resurrect him, he is liable. Rambam regards the resurrection of R. Eliezer as metaphorical, representing the resumption of the debate over the aknai oven (cf. Baba Mezi'a 59a) at a time when it was no longer appropriate, that is, after the majority had already decided, likening stubborn debate without legal justification unto a reanimated corpse deprived of the good inclination.

[28] cf. Megilla 7b.

[29] R. Abye, taking Raba literally, objects that since Zeira's resurrection was accomplished through prayer rather than magic, the problems discussed earlier do not apply. Raba responds by saying that Abye has only learned to eat bread, and not cake. According to Rashi, bread here represents serious study, while cake represents light-heartedness. According to the Tosafot, bread represents literal meanings, while cake represents the deeper metaphorical level. R. Abye has failed to apprehend that Rabba's compliment to Zeira is figurative rather than literal. Rabba was known for employing humor as a pedagogical tool, cf. Shabbat 30b.

[30] That is, this predatory behavior is typical of the Romans.

R. Shimon ben Gamaliel called together the men of the Academy. R. Phineas said, 'The kings of the earth set themselves against the LORD'[31]. R. Shimon ben Gamaliel however responded, 'Let all who take refuge in you rejoice'[32] – all who take refuge in you, not all who honour you. From this we learn that also the wicked must be protected in time of general calamity. Others say, not until they repent, as it is written, 'for you are my refuge; into your hand I commit my spirit'[33]; that is, only when they are sufficiently contrite.

While they were thus engaged, a great number of those [of whom it was said, it arises from the ground] 'OUT OF ITS PROPER TIME', approached the Academy to pursue [the people there]. R. Jose said, 'if your enemy is hungry, give him bread to eat'[34], and cast loaves before them, but they did not eat. R. Judah then said, 'at twilight you shall eat meat'[35], and he cast a hen before them. The pursuers devoured the hen. Then R. Nehemiah cast two ducks before them, and they devoured the ducks. Then R. Phineas cast three ewes before them, and they devoured the ewes. Then R. Nathan cast four goats before them, and they devoured the goats. Then R. Yochanan cast five calves before them, and they devoured the calves. He said, 'They slice meat on the right, but are still hungry, and they devour on the left, but are not satisfied.'[36]

Then R. Shimon ben Gamaliel cast six bulls before them, and they devoured the bulls. R. Phineas said, 'When they had eaten them, no one would have known that they had eaten them, for they were still as ugly as at the beginning.'[37] R. Judah said: May we also awaken![38] Then R.

---

[31] Psalm 2:2. In other words, we have no obligation to assist the Romans, our occupiers.

[32] Psalm 5:11.

[33] Psalm 31:4-5.

[34] Proverbs 25:21.

[35] Exodus 16:12.

[36] Isaiah 18:20.

[37] Genesis 41:21.

[38] The passage which R. Phineas cites, in which Pharaoh recounts his dream to

Judah cast seven oxen before them, and they devoured the oxen. Then R. Meir cast eight elephants before them, and they devoured the elephants. Then R. Shimon bar Yochai brought a Leviathan from the sea, and they devoured the Leviathan. At once they became so rotund that their bellies were like the wheels of a chariot, and the men of the Academy rolled them into the sea.

R. Eliezer ben Hyrcanus meanwhile entered the house of Acher to pursue him. Because Acher was unable to escape, he said: my master, I have a question about the [ritual purity of] ovens. Although R. Eliezer was compromised in his faculties, the matter interested him greatly, and so he ceased [to pursue].

Acher said: consider an oven like that of Aknai[39] which, in the year of the Destruction of the Temple, was used on the first day of Passover to store unleavened bread that had previously been wrapped in a cloth that was stained with the menstrual blood of the oven's owner[40], and the owner then purified only the parts that had been touched by the unleavened bread.

Now, consider that the mother of the owner was a proselyte; however, the rabbinical court which converted her had said: we will allow you to convert only under the condition that your parentage is pure.[41] But the proselyte's father had been a Jew who was conceived after his own father had given his mother a bill of divorce about which he said: this paper belongs to me, except under the condition that the Temple will be destroyed, God forbid, and that on the first day of the festival of Passover of that year, we will have a great-granddaughter who, G-d forbid, will

---

Joseph, is followed by, 'Then I awoke.'

[39] An oven composed of many parts; the debate about whether the whole, or only the parts, must be purified, led to R. Eliezer's excommunication, cf. Baba Mezia 59b.

[40] Which would render the cloth, and thus the matzah, and thus the oven impure, presuming the owner of the oven is Jewish.

[41] In other words, only if her immediate ancestry is free of illegitimate births; in this case, the legitimacy of her father is in question.

own an impure oven, in which case this paper belongs to you.[42] In such a case, is the oven pure or impure?

R. Eliezar said: it is pure! And with that he returned to dust.

Rava asked Raba: who is more to be praised, R. Meir, because he warned the Academy, or R. Shimon bar Yochai, because he brought the Leviathan? R. Abye objected: but perhaps Acher is to be praised, for his task was the greater?[43] Raba answered: R. Eliezar ben Hyrcanus is to be praised. At his second death, he remembered the Temple and turned towards Jerusalem, as we learned: IF IT FACES TO THE EAST.

---

[42] The divorce is valid only if the bill of divorce, including the paper it is written on, is given entirely to the wife. If the husband retains ownership, the divorce would be invalid, and thus the woman would be the legitimate offspring of the couple, and hence her daughter, the oven's owner, would be Jewish. cf. Gittin 84a.

[43] Because R. Eliezar was a more formidable threat than the others.

WISEMAN'S
TERROR TALES

ANNA TAMBOUR

Irving Wiseman's uncle Leo dropped some magazines on Irving's bed. 'Enough dreaming,' he said, pulling the book from his nephew's hands and placing it on the bureau. He would have liked to toss it, but it was a book, and even more than that, a library book.

'You gotta make a living,' he said.

Irving sighed, but rolled over and laid the magazines out before him on his bedspread like cards in a game.

'You got talent,' said Leo. 'You must have. So they're showing it, no?' He pointed like some professor in the movies at the middle magazine.

The right breast of the woman in the underwired but otherwise unstructured pink brassiere stared at the 17-year-old. It wasn't just the woman's youth that perked those breasts, Irving knew. His uncle had told him that 64% of women, once they hit the age of 20, already have bosoms that not only fail the pencil-test, but are as perky as easy-over-light fried eggs. This woman's bazoongas were held up in their most flattering form, high as they could go. Irving didn't know but guessed that the reason was those arms pulled up by wrists clamped into cuffs on that chain pulled over the swing-bar by the scientist's assistant.

Leo stabbed that cover – *Marvel Tales*, May 1940 – with his pipe. Ashes fell on the assistant's manic frown. 'What have you to tell me?'

Irving opened his mouth, looking ready to recite, or yawn.

'No, that's too easy,' said Leo. 'What does that remind you of? And this is no bordello. What you lying down for?'

Irving sat up and ran his hand through his thick curls. 'The other pink job.'

'And when are they not pink?'

'When they're red or chartreuse or – '

'If you can't piece these together, just how you think – '

The boy took off his glasses and pinched his nose, an odd gesture considering that without his horn-rims, he looked like Michelangelo's son of stone. 'Long blade of paper-guillotine in action of cutting a brunette in half. All right already. False underwire of round cotton-waste piping, non-adjustable rayon-satin ribbon straps, one-inch separator of same connecting bandeaux-style shallow unshaped cups. Suitable for women with no body who think they don't need fill. A Twenties look.'

'Better.' Leo produced yet another magazine from inside his fitted suit. 'This? I just picked it up.'

Irving pulled the magazine close to his face. Its ink was still loud, crude. Only out for a few months, this February 1941 *Spicy-Adventure Stories,* 'Space Burial', featured a screaming redhead slipping off the back of some flying bird – the important thing being that apricot sateen number with the shaped straps and wholly improbable way that the breasts could be supported. He snorted. 'Artistic license. No can do. Not with that fabric and no seams.'

'Now we're getting somewhere.' Leo pointed to the bed. 'What do you think of that one in the line-up?'

' "The Soul Scorcher's Lair"?'

The middle-aged man with no paunch waited. After all, he had once had dreams, too. But 15 seconds was enough.

'If you think I'll let a fantazyor eat your mother's kreplach. And she a widow working her fingers off...'

'Hot-formed lace, steel underwire, flare-banded from armpit to breast differentiators, elasticised arm straps, presumably three-hook back, D cup, black, suitable for full but firm breasts because there is still no adequate support for the average woman.'

'Excellent, my boy.' Leo smiled broadly, the picture of the proud uncle, even possibly, though he'd never seen it, the university professor gratified that his student had actually listened to all his lectures. Leo was proud of himself, too, for he had successfully hidden the hurt that the boy, through the callousness of youth, had dealt him. For Irving was right. That bra had been a great seller in '37 – but its success had rested on the racy lace and daring black. Women don't know how to fit a bra, and this one, for all its advertised appeal, was two flimsy colanders, so the average woman's breasts were sadly earthbound or showing their inadequacy of build with an embarrassment of collapsed cups when what they needed was adequate shaping, filling, engineering, uplift.

As Irving civilised his hair and washed his face and hands, he heard his mother setting the freshly scrubbed table in the kitchen – laying it with three places for the three people who lived in that little flat in the Bronx.

He was pleased in one way that he'd made Uncle Leo happy. Of course he didn't want to hurt the man – and besides, he felt sorry for him. But he also felt a simmering anger that he could hardly admit to himself. To sign his life away. Yes, so Mama had started in the sweatshops at the age of nine. But still. Irving put that out of his mind while he dried his face, and dreamed for another snatched moment of designing rockets.

What he knew of the breasts of the average woman, of any woman for that matter, was the sum of what he'd seen of Egyptian, Greek and Roman statuary in the Metropolitan Museum, all those magazines his uncle brought home for him to study, and Leo's own blueprints and lectures about the real things.

Irving wondered if the man, that lifelong bachelor, had ever touched the real things. He'd gone from being a tailor of men's suits, an unenviable specialty in New York in the 1930s, to a brassiere designer, only because of a friendship made by Irving's mother, who when her husband dropped dead of a heart attack when Irving was only 13, went into business on her own, sewing foundation garments to fit particular women, especially those with a breast or two cut off, and opera singers.

Her constructions, all made of pink canvas, could have held cement. Their fillings felt rather like it, and never shifted. Sometimes she made shapes that looked quite beautiful to Irving, but that she inevitably had to modify for her conservative clients, who seemed to prefer what Irving thought of as the 'squashed look'. Maybe they were ashamed. He didn't know but felt frustrated for his mother, who couldn't afford that luxury.

It was she who had talked to her brother about setting Irving up. She not only didn't have the money but there was also that limit of 'Hebrew' students already reached in all the top schools. So he had to take that job Uncle Leo wangled for him, opening in January. Until then, after graduation from high school in a week (what a waste of science classes!) he was to learn the trade – designing for three dimensions with two-dimensional materials, under her. Not that this training came, of course, with an opportunity to look at or touch the goods inside these constructions.

The first day on the job he successfully ran a Singer needle through his forefinger. It was a good lesson in driving speed on the newly electrified machine. After that, he surprised himself on the thing, finding that the more difficult the curves, the more fun he had making the turns, and he grew so skilled that his mother started trusting him with ever more mountainous jobs.

The fittings were all done in her bedroom, and the clients looked nothing like, say, that blonde with manacled hands and the rayon full-torso breast-delineating underpiping but otherwise purely unsupportive cups fronting *Terror Tales*, September 1934. Most of her clients were, frankly, variations on the potato or a cubist painting, even with her expert foundations giving them shape. 'Today's woman,' he said to her one day, 'should thrust out rockets, not your matzo balls.'

'So, Irving. This today's woman? She tells you this?'

Her son blushed reassuringly.

'You fantazyor,' she said, patting his cheek. 'Your today's woman is in the future, and she's made of steel.'

But to make him happy, she let him create two designs that were quite astoundingly shaped, giving body where needed he said, but always 'up and outlift'. She hated wasting the canvas and thread, but kept that thought to herself. After he had constructed both models – impeccably cut and sewn, she was pleased to note – she offered them to her two youngest clients, having quickly to explain that it was just an idea. She almost lost both women.

So instead, she asked Irving to tell her of his dreams while he sewed.

It helped him to hear her sigh.

The months passed more quickly than he imagined they would, and he was doubly sorry to see them go. His mother had always been a heroine to his way of thinking. One day he would find a woman like that, he thought when he forgot that he'd be a brassiere designer, something to laugh at. So embarrassed did he feel that he refused all comers, and with looks like his and his shy, thinker's manner, he could have explored all he wanted, even the nice girls.

December came, and with it, the Day of Reprieve.

He was told that there was no way he could get into the Air Corps, so he went to the Army office across the street, but after interviewing him the guy there after interviewing him, wrote something on a piece of paper and sent him back across the street. And he walked out of that office signed up for a course, launching him into the Air Corps.

With his new skills in map-making, he flew over Germany and then was stationed to Burma, where he learned to hate the English for their filled storehouses, meant not for the people who needed them, but for export; visited temples that he laughed to think about gracing towns in the US of A – the horror! And in this alien land he felt for the first time, the real things, if only stone; and after much encouragement and teasing, the real things with a real-life woman, who said she 'love' him, but she kicked his pet mongoose.

He hadn't been surprised that the stone women on the temples had matzo-ball breasts. After all, they were ancient, weren't they? But this woman in the flesh – hers were something he had only imagined. She was soft and warm, but they could have been made of tin, they were so conical. They only confirmed, however, his thoughts that the woman of today would love to look like that if she could. Of course, she must have been a freak, a beautiful one but nevertheless a fantasy come to life in flesh. Breasts like these didn't grow on women, or he would have seen them on statues. They needed guidance.

Not that he planned to give it to them. No siree. Now that he'd escaped, he saw – through the squalor of death and fear, the confusion of cruelties intended and unthinkingly dealt out, this war that he helped to serve – not only the opportunity but the responsibility to engineer a shining, uplifting future.

He was just having what isn't supposed to be but what many have experienced: a great war – when in a nightmare, a blonde turned up, 'Dead Man's Bride' from *Terror Tales*.

One pitiless noon he was sitting outside his tent, a wet kerchief over his head. He had been dreaming – but only daydreaming, and sketching rockets.

'Wise guy,' she cracked, as if that nut were fresh. She had a hand on her hip and one of those so-sure-of-herself voices that fit her cover-girl looks, on that cover. But she mustn't have travelled with a compact. Her peach-gold skin was pitted with oozing sores, one eye filled with dirt, and her skull poked out like the Andaman Islands, from a blue-tinged scalp.

91

Yes, Irv had been around. He noticed not only that, but that her breasts were like two flops of camp stew. Man, did she need engineering, and uplift.

She sidled around behind him and hung her head over his shoulder. 'That's what I want,' she said. 'We all want it.'

'This?' He drew the nose cone, then another one beside it, and drew straps.

'Exactly.' She snatched up the paper as something precious, and held it to her ravaged chest. He was almost charmed. And she didn't smell half as bad as other unexpecteds he'd come across, unreported 'casualties', the still oozing dead.

He wondered if someone had put her up to this. 'Do you know the woman in that black lace number in *Eerie* – '

'Corinne? She prayed for you! Thank her for your luck changing.'

He repressed a smile. He'd always reckoned this blonde for a tale-spinner, but it was flattering nonetheless.

'Can she come here?'

The earth moved, and up from it crawled Corinne. That bra had not lasted half as well as it should have. It was even less recognizable than Corinne.

But she retained some of her strawberry-blonde set hair. It had looked to be so shellacked that its preserved curves looked set for her to be displayed in a museum.

'Dis war will end,' she said through her lipless mouth. 'And you will become the greatest brassiere designer there ever was.'

He jumped up. They could have tossed a grenade in his lap, his heart pounded that bad. He wanted to flee into the jungle, but knew they'd follow. What did they have to lose? He couldn't lose them, so he said simply, like some dumb grunt, 'I'm sorry but I'm a rocket man.'

'Not on your life, you're not,' said the *Dime Mystery* Maid, now to his left. He looked her over, and was unsurprised to note that her flimsy slip of a bra, which couldn't hold two flies, had slipped to her waist. What with her ribs sticking out, and her breastbone and all, he had to remember what her problem was. Ah yes, no breasts to speak of.

Before the rest of his troop came back from manoeuvres, he was surrounded by a bevy of former cover girls, all insisting that he heed their call. Their story was that it was too late for them, but they still had their duty, which they would carry out no matter what.

'Not,' chuckled the siren named Mitzi ('of "Crisis in Utopia"', she reminded him) 'that "no matter what" means anything to us. We have forever. And a purpose in death.'

'But why should you care?'

'Haven't you noticed that we're all young dead?' said Mitzi. 'Models don't last long. But that doesn't mean we don't feel solidarity with the girls still walking the streets in flesh and bras. They don't want old-fashioned bodies. They don't want straps that fall down. They need up and outlift! And you're gonna give it to 'em, Captain.'

The girls, as they called themselves, gave her the best they could with a Bronx cheer.

They were more persistent than gunfire in an assault. And they didn't let up for sleep or regrouping. He'd seen so much already in this war that he didn't think them any more strange than some of the orders he'd been given by Command. Nor the sights that he came upon and helped to make, because of the orders from people whose war experience was intensely spent on maps only pocked by pins.

He argued with the girls. Then he tried to reason, telling them what a waste a creative brain like his would be – to engineer brassieres – when space (and the needs of war of the future) cried out for a genius with solutions.

'But you're such a genius in this,' said Corinne, giving her lacquered hair a flick, which exposed her shapely bones. 'Besides, you can't deny your heritage.'

'What's that s'posed to mean,' Mitzi shot.

'He's a Hebe, that's all. No offense, Mitzi, but you know.'

Mitzi would have flashed her eyes, but she couldn't even blink them. Instead, she said, 'Captain Wiseman. Irving. Be a doctor.'

'Or better yet,' piped up the woman who still had chunks of her zaftig build, dug into her terrible torture marks. 'A psychiatrist.'

So suddenly he had two allies, sort of.

And there was war amongst the girls till finally, he was shipped home, a month after the war officially ended.

The ship was crammed full of men, but that didn't stop the girls boarding too. They weren't alone. There was a whole contingent of dead with missions, attached to both troops and officers. Irving sensed this, though they were better at hiding than any soldier he'd ever known. He never talked about them to anyone, and no one told him of the dead who stalked them. Does it take war to bring them out, he wondered. And if so, could at least there be the retribution of having them pester just as much the idiots in Command, the civvies who made money from the war, or glorified all the wrong things about it. But he'd been around enough by now to figure that only soldiers were delivered these particular rations – these dead, all on missions.

So while the living had to come to terms with peace, war raged amongst the girls and at him – a constant ack-ack about his future, all the way to New York Harbour. But not one of them advocated rockets. Even to reminisce about riding them on covers, as (formerly) big-chested Bertha L'Amour had in 'Payload: Vavoom', rockets were a no-go zone. If he brought them up, the girls would sing Big Band hits – and with their torn-out and rotted voice boxes, now *that* was the stuff of nightmares.

So when he walked down the plank and saw his mother, shorter than he remembered, he strode up to her and hugged her long and hard, with a grip less manly than his looks. Then his uncle shyly shook his hand. Leo looked at him with awe, his mother with simple pride. Nothing more had reached them but the briefest 'I'm doing well. This land is beautiful' for years.

Two hours later, over the gefilte fish, he said to his uncle, 'There still a job working with you?'

'Irving.' His uncle placed his fork on the plate and wiped his mouth. 'Don't you dream any more?' He looked intensely at his fish. 'I'm sorry. I can only imagine what you've seen.'

'Leo,' Irving said. 'You've seen it too.'

Leo reached out and took his hand. 'You can come to work tomorrow. I'll make sure they take you. A veteran with skills.'

'Over my dead body,' said Bessie Wiseman, splashing the chicken soup. 'You must go back to school. That's an order, Rocket Man.'

And somehow, in that little apartment in the Bronx, the wind howled outside and the lift creaked with arthritis, but the girls couldn't get in. Out on the pavement this chorus of sirens pitched everything they had up at that window – wheedles, soft-soap, promises, demands – in brassy blare to rot-muffled croak, they threw their voices up at Irving, safe inside.

But they knew they'd been defeated.

And Irving Wiseman did become a rocket designer, a military scientist on typically low pay and sworn to secrecy about his achievements, but happy as clams are supposed to be, and they don't complain. A clam who didn't even notice, and was never told by his uncle, that while he was gone, the Conical Bra had come out, a great success, and from a competitor. It was engineered with military precision, even had maximum reinforcement.

When the girls found out, they felt so stupid about having missed it all, having gone on a mission to the other side of the world (that failed anyway) when all the action was happening at home, that they slunk back to their holes and never regrouped.

ZAYINIM

ADAM ROBERTS

1

Jonie stole one of Daniel's books. 'Borrowed', we might say; but she knew what stealing was, and she knew what she was doing. On the other hand, her mother was always pressing her to read books, and – to be truthful – there was little else to do. Jacob and the others were away, so the rest were supposed to lie low, which was the mostest BORINGness, and Jonie had read all her other books. So she snuck into Daniel's room. It was actually the cab of one of the trucks, but he'd hung up drapes and set up a bookcase and made it quite homely. She picked a likely looking codex, and danced back to her den.

The book was called *Beyond Good and Evil* by a guy called Nate Char – an American, presumably, by the name. The title promised a crime-and-punishment story, or (more exciting) a crime-but-no-punishment story. But actually it was all dense prose like this:

> *Assuming truth is a Jew – what then? Is there not reason to suspect that all philosophers, in so far as they were dogmatists, have known very little about Jews? That the terrible seriousness and clumsy importunity with which they have usually paid their addresses to the Truth, have been unskilled and unseemly methods for impressing the Jews? Certainly Truth has never allowed herself to be won; and at present every kind of dogma stands with sad and discouraged mien – IF, indeed, it stands at all!*

That was the point at which Jonie bailed. She threw the book on the floor and lay on her bed for a while, chewing her fingernails. She spent five minutes trying to nibble her two pinkie nails into talons, and then gave up on that and bit them both close to the finger. Then she leapt up. Ran, with the uncoiled sudden energy of bored youth, out of her room, past the fence and to where her mother was working.

'What's a philosopher?'

'Somebody who tries to fathom the universe,' her mother replied, without looking up.

Jonie waited. After a while she cracked. 'Don't you want to know why I asked?'

Her eyes still on what she was doing, her mother returned, 'Why did you ask?' in a level voice.

'I borrowed one of Daniel's books. It says that philosophers are in love with the Jews. So are they *not* Jews, these philosophers?'

'There have been many Jewish philosophers,' said her mother, with that particular tone in her voice that was the closest she ever came to laughter. 'But there have also been philosophers amongst the Goyim.'

'Zombies? *Zombies* want to fathom the whys of the universe?'

Her mother looked up, and angled her head. 'I didn't say there were any zombie philosophers'

'Isn't Goy another word for zombie?'

'No,' she replied, returning her attention to whatever she was writing.

Jonie waited an age in the ensuing silence – whole minutes – before the energy danced out of her. She pirouetted from one end of her mother's desk to the other, and back again. Her mother continued plugging away at whatever she was doing, undistracted. 'Is Daniel on the prim?' Jonie asked.

'Your uncle is on perimeter duty, I believe,' mother replied. 'Perhaps you wish to apologise for taking one of his books without asking his permission?'

'Later!' Jonie cried, and raced out of her mother's room.

Elisheva was on the main door, but she'd always had a soft spot for Jonie and didn't need much persuading. 'Take one,' she insisted, pressing a loaded bolt-gun into her hands. 'Remember: aim at the bluest eye.'

'Sure, yes, OK, of course, I *know*,' Jonie told her, in an ecstasy of impatience. Then the heavy triple-shield iron door grated noisily open and Jonie ran out into the sunshine. She didn't so much as look back at the compound; she just ran. Lay-low week take that!

The long grass hissed like snakes as she sprinted through it. She came out at the rise, and the lake was spread out all before her in the afternoon sunshine, each of the myriad wavelet inset with a pip of bright sunlight. To the left was a bole of willows, like a knot of giant green jellyfish trailing their tentacles in the water. Everything was pale green and dark green, and the water was blue-green, and Jonie ran in the sunlight direction: widdershins around the island. Down into a declivity, and up onto a small hill, and then she saw Daniel – dressed in bright red, standing like a flame in the field.

The red was on purpose, of course. The Zayinim were attracted to the bright colour, and would strut and stumble in Dan's direction, rather than bothering the compound. Of course, that put the pressure on Dan's marksmanship. But his marksmanship was fabled. Zayin was the Hebrew Z, Z-for-zombies, although it also meant *dick*, and lezayen meant *to insert the dick*, which Jonie thought was pretty funny, actually. Not that she had a whole lot of experience of dick, and still less of insertion. She hooted Daniel's name, and galloped so hard down the slope to him that she was out of breath by the time she arrived and it took her ages to get her breath back, and she had to lean her hands on her knees and face the ground like she was about to spew.

Daniel's creased face was trying to do stern. 'Shouldn't cry *out* like that, little one,' he told her. 'Shrieking. They're not deaf, you know.'

'To what do you owe the pleasure?' Jonie said. 'I'll tell you, Daniel. I read one of your books.'

'But I haven't written any books, Jonie,' said Daniel, genuinely puzzled.

'It was called *Better than Good and Worse than Evil*,' Jonie pressed. 'It's by an American, and it's about philosophers. It said philosophers were in love with truth, and also in love with Jews, and I figured that meant they *weren't* Jews. But who isn't a Jew? Apart,' she added, sweeping her right arm in a broadcast indicative gesture.

Daniel looked nervously around, in case one of them was slouching towards them. But the view was clear. 'Slow down,' he begged.

'A Zayin can hardly talk, and surely a Zayin can't write, so I'm thinking a Zayin can't be a philosopher. Thus and *therefore* I was wondering – since it's your book, you explain.'

When old Daniel frowned the three horizontal lines on his brow went, as it were, from normal to bold font; but more than that, two angled lines converging on the bridge of his nose sprang into visibility, like a giant V.

He holstered his gun, and pulled a long, sharp-ended stick from a loop on the other side of his belt. Jonie couldn't imagine what he was going to do with it, until he jabbed it hard into the soil, and then unfolded a sort of hinged canvas seat, no bigger than two cupped hands. He sat on this and took a breath. 'You're going too fast for me, child,' he said, and began extricating materials for smoking: a white tube the length of a live round; a lighter as red as his clothes. 'But the book is called Beyond Good and Evil, and it's not by an American. It's by a German, and it was very popular with the people who – ' And he nodded in the direction of the lake, to indicate all the Zayinim in their terrible masses, somewhere over there.

'No,' said Jonie, delightedly, 'kidding.' She flopped into the grass at her uncle's feet, and clutched her own knees to her chest. 'So it is a zombie philosophy!'

'No,' said Daniel, sounding now like a ventriloquist talking whilst simultaneously holding his cigarette between his lips. A click and the end became an ember. He breathed the smoke in deep. It made a loud, sibilant sound going in, like silk on silk. Then he let it out very slowly. 'It was written before that. But it inspired the people who made themselves into – that.'

'Wolf Hitler!' exclaimed Jonie, excitedly.

'He was one of them, one of the worst. But not the only one.'

'Tell me the story again,' insisted Jonie.

Daniel drew hard on his cigarette again, and breathed out a spear of smoke into the mild afternoon air. 'Well the Wolf hated Jews. And he was a ruler of Europe, and he made allies with others who hated Jews. And there was a big war; the whole world fought it. But the Wolves and the Bears banded together, and won that war.'

'If they hated the Jews, why didn't they kill them?' Jonie asked.

'They did. They killed the Jews in Europe, and Russia, and north Africa. There were other Jews in America, and although America lost that war and signed away reparations and agreed to,' Daniel coughed sharply, 'dis-ad-van*tag*eous trade agreements and so on, they at least kept their Jews.'

'What happened next?' Jonie pressed. She knew what happened next; but it was good to hear the story told.

'Well, the Wolf had a dream. He wanted to make a race of supermen, and this was because of books like the one you *stole* from my room, you know.' Jonie made a shocked face, but her uncle was smiling. 'The archetypal warriors, new warriors of a new war, were the überatmensch, and they were the prototype. That's what the writer of your book talked about,' (Jonie began to suspect he couldn't remember the guy's name) 'how to become more like the überatmensch, solitary hunters, utilising new technologies to destroy and inhabit new worlds and so on. Anyway. Anyway, the Wolf had the resources of the world at his disposal, so he made it come true. Through –' Daniel drew a curlicue of smoke in the air with his cigarette, gesturing at the vagueness of the next word '– science. Invincible warriors. Regenerating flesh, self-repairing gene-loads, immortality. *Beyond* mortality. And from a simple dose of a serum! So he dosed up an army and invaded China, and destroyed it. But it wasn't enough to give it to the army only – the people wanted it too. Everybody wanted it!

'The Wolf's allies begged for the serum, and he used it to force them to submit further to him. But eventually everybody got it. Everybody except the Jews. He agreed a treaty with America, and part of the agreement was: not the Jews. He thought – the Aryan Americans and the Spanish Americans and the Noble Native Americans will live forever in a warrior world, but the Jews will be mortal, and die out.' He was down to the stump of his cigarette now, and Jonie was impressed at the way he held the last bit of it with his nails, so it didn't scorch his skin.

'But we're still here.'

'Immortality is a bad idea. The body keeps going, but eventually the mind fall apart. The human mind isn't built to last forever, and eventually it curls up on itself and shrivels down. That's why the Zayinim are so... thoughtless.'

'That's because we shoot for their brains. We shoot their brains and they can't think. They don't die, but can't think,' said Jonie.

'Every human on earth was made a zombie, except the Jews!' said Daniel. 'You think that we shot every one of them in the head?'

'I can't believe everyone in the world was made a zombie,' challenged Jonie. 'There must have been thousands and thousands.' She remembered reading something about the pre-Zayin world. 'Millions!'

'Indeed. And a lot died in fighting over the serum. But a lot more got it – just not *us*, though. Then the new supermen and superwomen discovered that they couldn't carry children to term any more. The supermen could *plant* the seed like ever they did before, but the superwombs couldn't hold on to the babies. But they figured: I'm upset by this? Me? I'm immortal! And they lived to a hundred, and were still as young as when they took the serum. And then they lived to a hundred and twenty, and they were young. And then, at a hundred and fifty – don't ask me why, am I a scientist? – their minds started folding in on themselves, like a spider sprayed with water in the washtub. You've seen the way they're all legs and motion, and a quick slurp from the tap and they curl into a full stop?'

'Yes, yes,' said Jonie, impatiently. 'And?'

'And they all went the same way. Immortal, but thought-impaired. Stumbling about. Too stupid and disoriented to avoid banging into things. Like leprosy, they began to knock bits off. Even serum-repair don't cover everything – fingers regrow like courgettes; eyeballs grow back white as gobstoppers. And the Zayinim were too slow-witted to help themselves, stumbling about. The only thing they knew was: war. They'd been made as warriors. So they stumble about, and when they meet another of God's creatures they tear it to pieces! Which is why we have to keep them at bay. That's the definition of a warrior. A warrior is someone whose whole thought is: war.'

'Other people, apart from the Jews, must have resisted the temptation of the serum,' mused Jonie.

'You think we Jews *resisted* the temptation? We're such expert temptation-resisters? Don't be pumpkinny. If they'd've offered us immortality, wouldn't we have taken it? Only they didn't offer it. That was the deal. Because the Wolf hated us.'

For a while they sat in silence, looking at the lake. The little slurpy waves kept kissing away at the reed-bank, over and over. The sun was lower. Daniel pinched out the last quarter-centimetre of his cigarette, and brought up his tin. Then he placed the demi-stub on the metal, and lit it again with his lighter, bringing his face close to it to suck up the very last wisps of smoke. His cigarette tin was brushed with a score of black marks where he had done this before. But what can you do? Tobacco is precious.

'When did all this happen?' Jonie asked. 'I mean – I know it was a long time ago. I know it wasn't *living* memory.'

'My grandfather remembered those times,' Daniel said, musingly. 'He used to tell me about it.'

'He died. So that,' said Jonie, with the pedantry of youth, 'is not living memory.'

'He died, thank God!' agreed Daniel. 'There were a lot more of us, back then. Whole villages-full. Not like now. Ah well. Onward I suppose. Until we find the island and build the New City.' And he heaved himself off his stick-seat and folded it away.

2

That night Jonie had another go at reading the book; but it was indigestible stuff, and Daniel's handwriting didn't make it any easier – assuming it had been copied out by Daniel, and not some other scribe. His spelling was idiosyncratic even by Jonie's teenage standards, and sometimes his vocabulary was simply baffling.

> *Physiologists should think twice before positioning the drive for self-preservation as the cardinal drive of an organic being. Above all, a living thing wants to discharge its strength, to roll it forcefully from birth to death: life itself being fundamentally a Wheel to Power. Self-preservation is the oblique perversion of this wheel, the most frequent consequences of zombie life.*

Physical-what-nows? And then there was a series of weird proverbs, almost none of which made sense.

> *Anyone who despises himself will still respect himself as a despiser.*
> *It is the desire, not the desired, that we fall in love with.*
> *The consequences of our actions take us by the scruff of the neck, altogether indifferent to the fact that we have 'improved' in the meantime.*
> *We are punished most for our virtues.*

Vices, she presumed he meant to write there. And –

He who fights with monsters might take care lest he thereby becomes
a monster. And when you gaze long into zombies the zombies also
gaze into you.

Cold blue eyes. But, though young, Jonie had enough experience of the Zayinim to know that when they looked at you, there was nothing *behind* the look. They could not gaze. Most were repulsive-looking, but even the good-looking ones were no better than beasts: naked, filthy, dangerous. At breakfast the next day, she challenged Daniel: 'Do you write it out, Uncy? Is this book I *borrow-éd* in your handwriting?'

Daniel glowered at her. They were expecting Jacob back soon: later that day maybe, or maybe tomorrow, or the day after; and until he came back Daniel had to conserve his tobacco. Accordingly he was grumpy. 'You've a problem with my handy writing, maybe? Stealers can't be choosers, my girl.'

'It's hard going, and your spelling is a shocker, and I don't know,' Jonie said, haughtily enough. 'Tell you what the problem is? The problem is the book has no story.'

'No story,' snorted Daniel, rubbing the palm of his hand over his tall, lined brow. 'Stories you want, eh? But we're beyond stories now. The world has ended, and we're living in the afterwards, and there are no stories any more.'

Her mother nodded sagely at this, sipping her tea.

This was hardly a very satisfying answer, and Jonie vowed to give Daniel the book straight back – or burn it, or throw it in the lake, just to annoy him. But she didn't. She kept reading. There was something weirdly compelling in the mumbo-jumbo of it. And that night, as she drifted off to sleep, it occurred to her with a force like revelation – maybe this was a holy book. Maybe it contained the answer to the problems of the Jews and the Zombies.

She was jolted awake by raised voices. She knew immediately what the shouting meant. Sat straight up in bed. Slapped herself on the face. But she knocked her lighter on the floor when she reached for it, and wasting time scrabbling around before she could get a candle lit. Then she put shoes on, and put on her leather coat and gloves, the material stiff as thick cardboard in the cold. Cradling the candle she came out and along the corridor, and clanging up the metal steps to the top of the tower. Even before she reached the top she heard the *snap, snap* of rifle fire.

Everybody was there: her mother, Daniel, Elisheva, Esther, K. and Ash. K. swivelled the spotlight, and the others took turns at shooting at the indistinctness below. Ash handed Jonie a pistol (all the other rifles were away with father), but the moon was no bigger than a toenail clipping and some mocking clouds were playing peekaboo with even this small light. The Zayinim could be heard rather than seen, rattling the wire fence, making their distinctive 'ch' hissing noise, occasionally letting out dog-like high-pitched whimpers.

'It's not good, them being out at night,' Jonie gasped, excited despite herself. K. moved the spotlight, and three of them were visible in the circle. They turned their eyes up at the sudden illumination, and mother shot the one on the left – drove a groove right down the crown of its head, like parting its hair. It danced backwards as a spray of black fluid appeared above its head like a rooster's comb. Then it fell out of the light.

Abruptly, the Zayinim started shambling away. They were dumb, 'severely mentally impaired' as mother put it, but they were not wholly brainless. The fence was not giving way, and they weren't getting through. 'It's not good, that they're out at night,' Jonie repeated.

'Indeed not,' said Elisheva. Zombies usually got active in the warmth of the day. Unless they got food, that was the only way they *could* get active. Shambling around in the small hours must have meant they'd been feeding. And feeding carried with it the inevitable correlative: *feeding on whom?*

'I'm going to start one of the trucks,' said Daniel, heading down the stairs. 'We need more light.'

'Don't waste the petrol,' said mother. 'They're going anyway.'

'You sure?'

As if in answer to his question, clouds parted and enough pearl-coloured moonlight fell on the field in front of the camp to show it deserted.

'They're gone,' mother pronounced.

Jonie was sent back to bed, but of course she was too wired-up to sleep now. She read some more of the Char book, though reading by candlelight always made her eyes tired. Was Char really his name? Or was it a pseudonym. The only sure way to destroy one of the Zayinim was to burn it to ash; and in the latter days, when there had been end-times attempts to stem the tide of the zombermen, much of civilisation had gone up in smoke. Several times, when the camp had moved, Jonie had seen the scorched remains of cities, squares of slag where even weeds would not grow, black earth. It was why there were so few books. So little of everything. *The philosopher of the charred.* He had the answers! If only she could interpret the book aright.

> *The Jews — a people 'born for zlavery' as Tictacus and the whole ancient world says, 'the chosen people' as they themselves say and believe — the Jews achieved that miracle of revaluation of values thanks to which life on earth has for a couple of millennia acquired a new and dangerous fascination — their prophets fused 'rich', 'godless', 'evil', 'violent', 'sensual' into one and were the first to coin the word 'world' as a term of infamy. It is in this inversion of values ... that the significance of the Jewish people resides: with them there begins the slave revolt in morals.*

'Zlavery'? Was the word an artefact of Daniel's orthography? It wasn't in her Websters – she got out of bed and checked. So was it a slip of the pen? Or actually intended as a portmanteau of *zayin* and *slavery*? How were the Jews born for that?

She snuffed her candle and lay down again, until she felt sleep creep over her, like sinking into a hot bath. Then it suddenly shot through her mind, a fiery spear in her thoughts. They *were* slaves – slaves to the persistency and hostility of the Zayinim! A hundred disparate things fell into a gorgeous and meaningful pattern for the first time – with what splendour it all made sense. The Egyptian pharaoh undead mumzombie people keeping the Jews in bondage until the red sea of blood opened its doors across charred black sands and they fled along the Mobius-strip pathway of DNA. The struggle between Jews and zombies would drag on, itself zombie-like, unless they found a way to pass beyond Jews and Zombies. The future. She was the future. New blood, and a new beginning. Breaking the old wheel of tradition. Helix and double-helix, and the doubling was a necessary part of the helix.

She debated with herself whether to get up, relight her candle, seek out her mother and explain things – but she could anticipate the cross temper of waking her at this hour. She'd explain it all in the morning. And, giving herself permission, she fell into sleep.

3

In the morning she woke with a fizzing in her stomach. But when she got up, and as she was rinsing her face in the basin outside, it dawned on her that she had *forgotten* the whole glorious unified vision she had had in the night. She sat on the end of her bed and waited for the inspiration to return to her, but it didn't. Then she grew angry with herself for slothfully falling asleep instead of getting up and doing something. Anything! Writing it down, shouting it in Daniel's ear. She propped her pillow against the end of the bed and punched it for a while. But that didn't do any good. Oh, she was in a foul temper went she went through to see what there was for breakfast.

Everybody was there, and they were right in the middle of a discussion about moving the camp. 'Include me out of this discussion, why don't you,' she wailed.

'We didn't want to wake you, princess,' said Ash, separating his beard into two forks that he plaited round one another, undoing the plait and smoothing the beard into one again – a nervous tick of his.

'We can't move until Jacob gets back,' said Daniel.

Jonie scowled at him. 'Of course we can't,' she said, sarcastically. 'We need the extra hands to help us load the trucks.'

'I didn't mean that,' said Daniel.

'He didn't mean that,' mother echoed.

'Then what did he mean?' snapped Jonie. And as she asked the question she saw, with a horrible internal clatter, what he meant. He meant: what if the others *don't* come back? What if they can't? She saw it. Those Zayinim from the night before had been eating something.

Her thought processes must have been obvious, because A. said, 'I'm sure they chanced upon a deer, or a sheep, or something.'

109

Jonie announced: 'Father is fine. And I've been reading Daniel's book, and I have had a vision. A vision! I suddenly saw how we could escape the predation of the Zayinim!'

Everybody was looking at her now. 'All right,' prompted her mother. 'How?'

'Actually I can't remember now,' she said, trying to look dignified. 'But I'm sure it'll come back to me.' She took a mug of porridge from the breakfast pan and retreated to her room to read more of the Char. But her attention jittered over the words, and she kept trying to cast herself back into the middle of the previous night.

> *...be assigned to pretence, to the will to delusion, to selfishness, and cupidity. It might even be possible that WHAT constitutes the value of those good and respected things, consists precisely in their being insidiously related, knotted, and crocheted to these evil and apparently opposed things – perhaps even in being essentially identical with them. Perhaps! But who wishes to concern himself with such dangerous 'Perhapses'! For that investigation one must await the advent of a new order of philosophers, such as will have other tastes and inclinations, the reverse of those hitherto prevalent – philosophers of the dangerous...*

It was no good. She couldn't concentrate. There was some commotion outside, so she gave up on her reading. She put on her jacket and gloves and hat and went to the main gate.

'There's one left over from last night,' said Esther, excitedly. 'They're all out there now sorting it out.'

'Let me through,' Jonie demanded.

'Your father wouldn't want me to.'

Esther was, like, a hundred years old. 'Don't be a shrivelled old *stupid* person, Esther, and let me *out*.'

'I'll tell him it wasn't my idea,' Esther grumbled. 'Take a gun, at least.'

'Yes yes yes,' said Jonie, snatching the weapon and squeezing through the door before it was even a quarter open.

It always felt good to be outside. Spring was everywhere now, which was good in one sense – no more sleeping in all her clothes wrapped in two blankets and still shivering with the cold – and very bad in another. The Zayinim became much more active in the warm months of the year. Not just in terms of moving more rapidly and with more purpose – although until you'd seen a zombie immediately after a feed you had no idea just how quickly they could go – but in terms of aggregating into larger and therefore more dangerous packs. Nonetheless, it was good to breathe the fragrant air.

Someday, she mused, she would escape it all. Start her own life. Have kids, maybe. Except that having kids would not be to escape.

They were all standing, a circle of folk in the long grass. It was indeed one of the Zayinim from the previous night – the one mother had shot across the top of its skull. It was lying on its back in the grass. Jonie came up behind Daniel, and then peered past him.

It was naked, as all the Zayinim were. Their bodies long outlasted whatever clothes they had once worn. This one was nude, but not all of them were – some were covered in hair, like beasts of the field. The thing was the serum, or whatever it was, that made them immortal. It prompted regeneration of the flesh, with almost miraculous speed and accuracy. But the accuracy was not perfect, and over long enough stretches of time weird glitches worked their way into the operation. This could take any number of forms, but a common one was that hair follicles grew thicker and thicker hair. Not this guy, though: he was bald, eyebrowless, pubic-nude and stark as a skeleton. But there were other oddities. At some point in its long life the zombie had been split open across the side. This wound had, of course, healed; but teeth had grown in an irregular pattern along the scar. It had only a finger and a thumb on its right hand, but its left hand was a root-tangle of extra fingers all clutched together. She couldn't help looking at its genitals: a smaller penis grew from the end of its actual penis, the way potato-buds sometimes sprouted from whole potatoes. The gouge carved by mother's bullet, an inch deep at its deepest point, divided its cranium along a black crease. But it still had both its eyes, and its mouth was working. 'Ch-ch-ch.'

'Burn it,' said K. 'The grass is spring grass, the fire won't spread.'

'Waste the petrol?' returned Ash.

'Jacob will be back soon,' said K. 'The others will be back soon. They'll bring more.'

'And if they don't?' Ash replied, adding hastily, lest he be misunderstood, 'Don't bring more *petrol*?' In case anybody thought he meant *don't come back*.

'We can't just leave it here,' said Daniel. 'I'll get an axe, take its head off.'

'There's another!' called Elisheva, pointing. Everybody looked. Not one but two Zayinim were shuffling round the margin of the lake. Further off were half a dozen more, also approaching. With a nice sense of the incipiency of the drama, the breeze suddenly woke up. It began shaking the willows, which moved their branches sluggishly as if waving the people away. There were, of course, no birds.

'Back inside,' said Daniel, aiming his bolt-gun downwards. 'I'll try and take out the rest of this one's brains.'

The others started back towards the camp. Ash started off first, and straightaway, with a booming yell, he fell. The long grass swallowed him. 'There's one here!' he hollered.

Daniel reacted quickest, leaping nimbly over the supine zombie at his feet and hurrying to Ash. There was a jarring bang as he discharged his weapon, and the next thing Jonie saw was Ash being helped back to his feet, blood all over his old head.

'They're in the grass,' mother cried. 'Scores of them! They've been creeping up!'

'Back to the compound,' bawled Daniel. He turned, and shot again at the ground. 'They're everywhere.'

Jonie felt her heart go dabbity-dabbity in her chest. She set off running for the compound, but at once the whole world swung about the axis of her right ankle, and the earth smacked her hard in the face. It took a moment to comprehend what had happened. Grabbed. Its undead hand around her ankle. She twisted in its grasp, aimed her weapon and fired it – missed. Its ghastly bifurcated head turned to her, and its mouth opened. She saw then that its teeth were not teeth at all, but fingernails.

'It returns,' the creatures hissed at her, in weirdly accented English. 'Eternally it returns. And – '

Her second shot did not miss.

112

The zombie flopped back, its whole face horrible compressed and distorted where the bolt had punched its way in, at the mid-point of its nose. But it did not let go its grip. She put the gun down to free both hands, and tried to prise the fingers off. The creature was still moaning, or trying to make words, or something – but its fingers were set like a stone bracelet around her leg. It twitched and tried to rise again, and Jonie felt a nauseous sense of panic coil in her stomach. The creature's free hand grabbed her left wrist. With her right hand she scrabbled behind her for the bolt gun – but with only one hand she could hardly reload it. Shuffling her position, she tried to bring her feet to bear. To kick out. The thing's mouth was still going. 'It,' it hissed. 'Always,' it hissed. 'Returns,' it hissed.

Drums sounded, or maybe it was an earthquake. Sunlight flashed, as if her soul were leaving her body. But she was free, and she hauled herself backwards. The light flashed again. The drums were the hoof beats of a horse, and her father was on the horse. The flash was his sabre, cutting through the two arms of the Zayin.

'Go,' he bellowed.

She got up and began running, still wearing the clamped hands of the creature, one on her wrist, one by her elbow. The only thought in her head now was to get back to the gateway. When the force caught her and lifted her from behind she did cry out, terrified that another one of the beasts had her. But it was her father, hoisting her up into the saddle behind him, as they galloped over the undulating ground.

4

For several hours they were all too busy in defence for thought. Jacob's party had not found any petrol, but the assault was on such a scale as to necessitate using their flame-throwers anyway. Ash cut away the two still twitching hands from Jonie, and burnt them in the fireplace. Then she went and took her place in the tower with most of the others, and picked her shots, and tried not to think about how horrible her experience had been.

By dusk the assault had been beaten back. The scale of it was alarmingly unprecedented: dozens of zombies, coordinating their attack. 'Not so stupid,' said Esther. 'I've always said so.'

'One spoke to me,' Jonie said, but nobody seemed to hear, and she didn't press the point. Because, once she'd said it, it sounded stupid. How could they *speak*?

'They followed us back,' said Jacob. 'They tracked us. We rode day and night, and day again, and they followed the whole way.' How tired he looked! 'And more will be along soon. We have to pack up. We must go.'

He had departed with three men and three women. The women were all right, but only two of the men returned. This fact only occurred to Jonie after sunset, when everybody gathered in the yard to wash and snatch food under the spotlight. 'Where's Beuys?' she asked.

Nobody answered this question. A particular answer would have been worse than no answer. It wasn't as if they needed to ask, actually.

Daniel was sitting on his strange shooting stick, smoking. So clearly Jacob had found some supplies, including tobacco. But no petrol. 'It's getting harder and harder to forage round here,' said Charley, one of the women in the party. 'We're going to have to move.'

Feeling bitter and angry and weary and depressed Jonie went back to her room. As if calling the back of a truck with tarpaulin for a ceiling a 'room' made it one! Her mouth was full of ashes. It was pointless. They should give up. What was the point in going on?

She slept for a while, and woke up from a nightmare, and slept again. In her dream she heard hoof beats again, but it was not her father's horses; the horses themselves were undead, chasing her down. She was running through long grass, and the undead horses were just behind her. She had time to think: they must have tried out the serum on animals as well, there must be zombie animals as well, when she woke sharply.

'Jonie?'

It was her father's voice. The hoof beats were him knocking on the slats at the end of the truck. He always knocked, politely, before disturbing her in her room.

She put her head out. The sky directly above was pre-dawn pale, mother-of-pearl, and a broccoli-bunch of rainclouds was squatting by the horizons. 'Dad,' she said, and jumped down.

114

Jacob was not a great one for hugs, but he clapped hands to her shoulders and kissed her quickly on her forehead. 'I'm sorry,' he said. 'It was such chaos yesterday, I did not have the chance properly to greet you.'

She looked around: everybody was busy. They were packing up. 'Do we have somewhere *actually* to go?' she asked. Her voice was still croaky with sleep.

'We cannot stay here,' replied Jacob, nodding slowly. 'Come. We foraged some coffee.'

'What a treat!' she said; and then felt immediately sorry for looking forward to the coffee when Beuys was dead.

'I will take a cup with you, my daughter,' said Jacob, with characteristic pompousness, 'and then we must both help with loading the trucks.' He was looking old, Jonie thought. Everyone around her was old. Except Beuys, and he wouldn't get any older..

Somebody had already folded away the tables, and stacked them ready for loading. But between them, Jonie and her father pulled out the legs and set one up again. Jacob poured two cups of coffee, and stirred in sugar, and they sat at the table opposite one another and drank.

Behind her father, away to the east, the rim of the world was starting to glow red. The sun returning. The sun always returned. But then, so did the night. That was the nature of *return*.

'I've been reading one of Daniel's books,' she told him, unsure what else to say. Obviously it was impossible to talk about Beuys.

'Oh yes?'

'I think it has the answer,' she told him, and as soon as the words came out she felt their infinite foolishness.

'The answer to what?' her father asked, with ingenuous seriousness.

She couldn't back away now. 'To all this. To us, and to – them.'

Jacob raised one of his impressively horticultural eyebrows. 'There's an answer?'

'We have to go beyond us and them,' she said, uncertain where the words were coming from, or where they were going. 'It's always the same thing, and that's a kind of slavery. The struggle to turn the wheel is a kind of slavery. We have to break the wheel. Or – no, wait. Unpack it, unroll it. Squirl it out into a moebius strip. Or …' She took refuge in the mug, and drained the last of the coffee. Some of the sugar had formed a crusty sludge at the bottom, and she dipped her pinkie finger into this. 'When we fight the Zayinim, we become Zayinim. The difference between us and them is that we can choose *not* to be Zayinim. But that means going beyond the fight. Making peace of some kind.'

The eyebrow was still up. Behind Jacob the sky was starting to acquire the same golden-brown sweetness as she knew the sugar possessed. The storm clouds were away to the north, and – who knows? Maybe they would stay there. The light that suffused the heavens was also in her bloodstream now.

'We can't go on like this,' she said.

The eyebrow came down. She had said something to which her father could relate. 'We cannot,' he agreed.

They were silent for a while, and the sky grew more gloriously honeyed in its clarity.

'Daughter,' said Jacob, putting the cup down. 'I have rebuked Esther.'

'It wasn't her fault,' Jonie said, automatically.

'She should not have let you out. I have rebuked her, and she assures me she will not be similarly delinquent in the future.'

'Dad!' Jonie squealed. The sunlight had vanished from inside her. Now she felt only resentment and a kind of dull panic. Stuck inside! Stuck inside for ever.

He held up his hand. 'We cannot afford to take risks with you, daughter. You are the future. The only future.' He meant babies, of course. She hated when he referred to this, although he was never very explicit. She hated the sense of responsibility, not just for her, but for the whole of humanity. 'Which brings me to my news: we met another tribe.'

This was huge news. 'You did?' A whole new group of people? Some handsome young guy her own age?

'Not a large tribe, and with no... no young people, I'm afraid.'

This was a disappointment. 'None at all?'

'I'm sorry. But they said they had heard tell of a larger community, away to the north on the coast. My worry is that we lack the petrol to move the whole camp there. But we must try. The island...'

The island was Jacob's long-term plan: to move onto an island large enough to support them, cleanse it of any Zayinim that might be there, and build a New Jerusalem. But there was no point in doing that with only 13-year-old Jonie old enough to bear children, and the only men around capable of impregnating her close family. The goal was to gather together a viable number of different families, including youngsters. That had been the goal for as long as Jonie could remember. With the certainty granted only to the very young, she was convinced it would never come to anything.

'We must look to the future,' he said.

Jonie wanted to reply: yet we spend all our time looking to the past! But the sun had risen now, and he was standing up, so she stood up too. They washed the cups together, and folded the table away. 'The youngest,' Jacob said, 'was fifty-nine.'

'The youngest?'

'Of the tribe we met. Seven people – not a viable number. Two women in their seventies, the rest old men. My age, or older. The youngest was a man called Ephraim, and he was fifty-nine.'

With that he went off to help Daniel and mother with the crane on the back of the biggest truck, to move the fence portions. Jonie went off to help the others, packing trunks, checking the horses were all right. It only occurred to her much later that Jacob might have given her that information because some manner or type or kind of discussion had taken place about wives and husbands. Who else but her as the wife? But the very idea was so ghastly she put it away, behind her, and refused to think of it. There was a needle voice, inside her head, and it went: *what's the alternative, ducky? What's the alternative, my little brood mare?*

What's the beyond? Good question.

They were halfway through packing the fence portions onto the big truck, and had folded down the tower into its lorry-back, when Ash called out that he could see Zayinim in the field.

It was a horribly vulnerable time for them to attack, but sometimes it happened that way. Daniel, father, mother and K. mounted their horses and rode off as the others doubled their efforts. The sky brightened with early morning, and then darkened again as the rainclouds rolled over. Half an hour after setting off, the rider returned.

'Something off,' mother told the group. 'We put a few down, but they're not attacking.'

'Why not?' K asked.

'Never mind why not,' Daniel called. 'Let's just get packed up and head out before they change their minds.'

They finished up the fence sections just as the first rain began to fall. They air chilled and went bluer than before, and big nut-sized raindrops splattered onto the dusty windscreens and dry tarps. Within moments it was a heavy downpour, lines sketching the air all around, hissing hard into the long grass with the sound of somebody frying up food.

They tied down the last of the cargo, hitched the cart to the back of the smallest lorry, tethered the horses behind the medium truck and set off. Jonie rode in the big truck; mother driving, with Daniel and Esther. They had to wait a minute because the steaming bodies of the passengers misted up the windshield, and they had to run the air-blowers to clear their view. But eventually they were off, driving in first-gear (as always), moving forward at a horse's walking pace.

The drove through the grass easily enough, and had an alarming moment going up the slope when the wheels slid intermittently on the new mud. But they crested the top, and if the big truck could do that, the rest would manage.

It was true, though: the field was full of Zayinim. It was the weirdest thing. Indeed, in all her short life Jonie had never seen anything like it. Two rows of zombies formed a kind of blank-eyed honour guard as they drove down the middle. They made no attempt to attack. They did not move at all, in fact. At one point Daniel climbed into the roof of his cab and put a few down with his rifle, but mother called to him to stop – why antagonise them? And they didn't seem bothered.

The clocklike tick and tock of the windscreen wipers.

Jonie watched. This one tall, hirsute, with too many ears and the arms hanging at his sides so long they reached almost to his ankles. This one had been a woman once, naked, with her skin covered either in scales or perhaps boils, Jonie couldn't see very clearly. This one stocky, muscles, with fangs like a tiger poking through the skin of his lips. This one black, this one white, this one with a third arm sprouting from a cankerous looking mass on its shoulder, this other long and smooth and genital-less as a doll. All standing, and just watching them as they rolled by.

'Spooky,' opined Esther.

The rain stopped. Soon enough the clouds moved away, and the sun came out.

'I'm always struck,' said mother, as the steering wheel, 'that the earth must be heavier after a rainfall than it was before. Isn't that a striking thought?'

Finally they reached the end of the Zayinim row and passed it, and left the whole grisly crew of them far behind. But the very last individual was the most unsettling of all, for he was dressed in clothes. They cannot have been the clothes in which he had dressed before; for those threads must have long since crumbled to powder. He must have dressed himself – or been dressed. Of all the zombies she had seen, he was the least deformed (unless the deformities were hidden beneath the clothes) – a stack of white hair on his head, and an ageless face. In the sunlight his eyes glinted a clear blue, and he looked straight through the window at Jonie with what seemed like intention. But it can't have been – of course. He almost looked handsome. If he hadn't been a zayin, he would have been handsome: with his strong nose, and white-blond hair, and primrose eyes. His head turning slowly, so that his gaze could follow her. A *dressed* zombie? Wearing his smart suit, and gazing forlornly as the squire's own daughter passed by. I mean, obviously not that. *Obviously* not. But it was weird.

'Have you ever seen them act like that before?' Jonie asked Daniel.

'They act weirdly,' was Daniel's opinion. 'Weird is the height and breadth and depth of them.' To celebrate the fact that they'd gotten away without further mishap he took out a cigarette and lit it. His sigh of contentment was not the sort of noise a human usually made.

It was hard for her to put the intensity of the creature's blue gaze out of her head. So she took out the book, the Beyond book, from the inside of her leather jacket, and tried to settle to reading it again. There was an answer in there somewhere, she knew.

CONTRIBUTORS

RENA ROSSNER is a graduate of the Writing Seminars program at The Johns Hopkins University, Trinity College Dublin and McGill University. She works as a foreign rights and literary agent at the Deborah Harris Agency in Jerusalem. Her poetry and short fiction has been published in a variety of online and print magazines and journals. Her cookbook, *Eating the Bible*, was recently published by Skyhorse Publishing.

OFIR TOUCHE GAFLA was born in 1968 in Israel. He has written five novels (*The World of the End, The Cataract in the Mind's Eye, Behind the Fog, The Day the Music Died* and *The Book of Disorder*) that garnered great acclaim. He won the Geffen and Kugel awards for his first novel and in 2014 won the Creation award for Writers. He has also written numerous short stories which featured in different anthologies and magazines. He teaches creative writing at Sam Spiegel School of Film in Jerusalem, and is currently a visiting professor at the University of Texas in Austin.

SHIMON ADAF was born in Sderot, Israel, in 1972 to parents of Moroccan origin. He began publishing poetry during his military service. Later, he moved to Tel Aviv and joined a rock band as songwriter and acoustic guitar player. He published three poetry collections and six novels so far. His third collection of poetry *Aviva-No* won the Yehuda Amichai Poetry Award in 2010. between 2010-2012 he published the Rose of Judea trilogy, which deals with the issue of Jewish identity in different realities and with the role of poetry in initiation to adult life. The second volume of the thematic trilogy, *Mox Nox*, won the Sapir Prize (the Israeli equivalent of the Booker Prize) in 2011. The novel *Sunburnt Faces* came out in English in 2013 (PS Publishing). He resides in Tel Aviv and teaches Creative Writing and Literature in Ben Gurion University.

DANIEL POLANSKY is the author of the Low Town fantasy noir trilogy. His next book, *Those Above*, will be released by Hodder and Stoughton in 2015. He is sometimes in Brooklyn.

SARAH LOTZ is a screenwriter and novelist with a fondness for the macabre and fake names. Among other things, she writes horror/thriller novels under the name S.L. Grey with author Louis Greenberg, a YA pulp-fiction zombie series with her daughter, Savannah, under the pseudonym Lily Herne, and quirky erotica novels with authors Helen Moffett and Paige Nick under the name Helena S. Paige. Her latest solo novel, *The Three*, was published in May, 2014. She lives in Cape Town with her family and other animals.

BENJAMIN ROSENBAUM's stories have appeared in F&SF, Strange Horizons, Harper's, and Nature, nominated for the Hugo, Nebula, Sturgeon, BSFA and Locus Awards, and been translated into more than 20 languages. He has been a party clown, rugby flanker, synagogue president, and programmer for the Swiss banks. He currently works in Washington, DC with his wife Esther and his kids, Aviva (author of the blues song 'Homework') and Noah (author of the RPG 'Galaxy World'). He is writing a roleplaying game about the fantastic shtetl, called *Dream Apart*.

ANNA TAMBOUR's fiction is always 110+% true tales, minus the names. Tambour's last novel, *Crandolin*, was shortlisted for the World Fantasy Award. Her collection, *The Finest Ass in the Universe*, came out in 2015 from Twelfth Planet Press.

ADAM ROBERTS has published fifteen science fiction novels and many short stories, some of them collected in *Adam Robots* (Gollancz 2013). He is a university academic as well as a writer, and lives a little outside London.

LAVIE TIDHAR is the author of *A Man Lies Dreaming*, *The Violent Century* and the World Fantasy Award winning *Osama*. His other works include the Bookman Histories trilogy, several novellas, two collections and a forthcoming comics mini-series, *Adler*. He currently lives in London.

REBECCA LEVENE has been a writer and editor for twenty years, working in the games, publishing, TV and magazine industries. Her new four-part epic fantasy series, The Hollow Gods, launched in July 2014 with *Smiler's Fair*.

Mosac (British charity No: 1139077) provides practical and emotional support to non-abusing parents, carers and families of children who have been sexually abused.

The charity was formed in 1992 when four mothers whose children were abused came together and drew strength from each other's shared experience and realised the need for a similar service for others.

Based in Greenwich in south London, Mosac offers a national helpline, as well as counselling, advocacy, support groups and play therapy, and aims to break the silence surrounding child sexual abuse by raising awareness through training and consultancy.

Proceeds from the sale of this book will be donated to Mosac.

www.ingramcontent.com/pod-product-compliance
Lightning Source LLC
Chambersburg PA
CBHW030352180626
46812CB00007B/2857